CRESCENT STREET

CRESCENT STREET

Set in London's impoverished and crime ridden East End—a tale of ruthless ambition, tragedy, love, and revenge.

A NOVEL BY
TERRY BUSH

ISBN: 978-1545440247

This book is dedicated to my wife, Sandra, our two sons, Ben and James, and our daughter-in-law, Teresa.

Also: in loving memory of my parents, Kathleen and Leslie.

ACKNOWLEDGMENTS

I would like to thank Jill Dawn Morris for her invaluable advice.

CHAPTER 1

The Sunlight Club in London's docklands was filling up quickly. Saturday lunch times were nearly always busy. Many of the regulars arrived earlier than usual as they wanted to get a close up look at the new performer who was slated to appear. By twelve-fifteen, the damp, dimly-lit dining area had filled with cigarette smoke and every seat was taken. Those left standing at the back of the room jostled for a view of the upcoming attraction.

The red light inside the dressing room flashed three times, indicating that the first act would commence in two minutes. Daisy swallowed the remaining drops of the large gin she'd poured earlier. She glanced in the mirror to ensure that her wig and face makeup were still in good order. When she made her way toward the waiting area her stomach began to churn. Her instincts told her to turn and run, but she knew there was no going back now. Moments later the curtains opened, the spotlights came on, and the gramophone started to play. Daisy pursed her lips to force a smile. Gingerly, she stepped onto the stage, her hourglass figure causing loud whistles as she began her routine.

The six-minute act felt like an eternity to Daisy, with her self-esteem withering steadily. Finally, the curtains closed to wild cheers and applause. Daisy grabbed her robe, wrapped it tightly about her body, and hurried back to the dressing room. She poured another nip of gin and downed it in one mouthful. Then she slumped onto the sofa and burst into tears.

Seeing Daisy's distress, a fellow performer sat beside her and took hold of her hand. "It's all right, luv." She said warmly, "Believe me, the first time is always the worst. In any event you must have done a good job; just 'ark at them Johnnies cheering for you."

"Thank you," Daisy whispered through the teardrops streaming down her face.

The young girl stroked Daisy's cheek while reflecting on her own experience. She had been performing for almost a year, but the overwhelming emotions she had encountered when stripping in front of a live male audience for the first time were still fresh in her mind.

CHAPTER 2

Derek Taylor examined the jewelry that he and his team had stolen the previous evening. He was pleased. He knew it was never a good idea to get greedy, and smart to only take items that were easy to sell and difficult to trace. His father was a living testament of what could happen if you didn't stick to this philosophy. Three stretches in the slammer provided ample proof of this.

Derek planned to eat lunch at his local pub on Crescent Street, then take a few samples of his newly acquired wares to show his mate, Mickey Dodd. Though Mickey was a local, he generally operated around the Piccadilly Circus area. "Never piss on your own doorstep" was his byword.

Mickey liked the goods and offered his most favorable terms. "I'll either take half for sixty percent of gross, payable when I've sold them, or I'll have the lot at my risk for forty percent of standard valuation." While Derek occasionally indulged in a wager on the horses, when it came to the disposal of "hot booty," his motto was: "A bird in the hand is worth two in the bush."

Derek's outlook on life was both clear and simple. He sincerely believed that he'd been put on earth for the sole purpose of enjoying himself. Work was to be avoided whenever possible—and his "business" was just a means to support the end goal. His pleasures included nice meals out, donning fashionable clothes, watching or playing football, propping up a bar 'til closing time, and at the weekend, having his way with any available floosy.

On the subject of women, Derek saw a parallel to his razor blades. It was always preferable to have a shiny new one, but their useful life was limited, and they had to be disposed of eventually. Further justification of this viewpoint was his strong dislike of the lovey-dovey attitude women invariably adopted after sex. He'd never comprehended why they didn't just roll over and go to sleep, or better still, fuck off home.

Following his get-together with Mickey, Derek remembered being low on cigarettes, so he stopped off at the corner tobacconist. "Can I help you, sir?" the assistant asked.

"Hello darling. Twenty Senior Service, please."

Derek eyed up the young girl as she retrieved his order from the display shelf. The white smock covering her street clothes did little to enhance her femininity. At the same time, it didn't disguise her ample bosom. "That will be ten pence, please," she said, handing over the white packet with its distinct naval insignia.

Derek placed a half-crown piece on the counter. "Are you new here, sweetheart? I drop by regularly. Unless I'm mistaken, I've never had the pleasure."

"That's probably because I only started two weeks ago," she replied, counting out his change.

Sure that the assistant was still in her teens, Derek remembered a line that he'd used successfully in the past. "If I wasn't certain you already had a boyfriend, I'd invite you to join me at the cinema this weekend."

The assistant restrained herself from giggling. She thought her customer was quite handsome, and she was enjoying his flirtation. However, she was also aware of the need to behave appropriately and avoid putting her job at risk. "I don't have a boyfriend," she said, checking to see that the shop manager was out of earshot.

Derek grinned. "In that case, can I interview for the position?"

The assistant glanced across to the confectionary counter where the manager was serving another customer. She leaned forward and said in a soft voice, "Look, I can't talk right now, or I might get myself into hot water."

Reading the situation in front of him, Derek asked, "What time do you finish work?"

"Five o'clock," she whispered.

"I'll meet you outside shortly afterward, then. By the way, my name is Derek Taylor."

"And mine's Daisy Walters," the assistant replied. Derek winked and strutted out the door wearing a smug smile.

For the remainder of the work day, Daisy was pre-occupied, reliving her brief encounter with Derek. Not only did she think he was handsome and amusing, she also liked the way he dressed. Her interest in boys had grown considerably in recent years, though due to family circumstances, she'd seldom been on a date. Shortly after Daisy's twelfth birthday, her father had died unexpectedly from a heart attack. The shock of his sudden death had a profound impact on Daisy's mother who quickly became fragile. This in turn led to ailments that often confined her to bed. Being the only child, Daisy had since spent most of her free time attending to household duties and caring for her mother.

Deep in thought, Daisy was brought back to the moment when the clock chimed five times. She put on her cardigan, wished the manager goodnight, and stepped outside. Searching the street in all directions, Daisy felt a wave of disappointment sweep over her when there was no sign of Derek. Marching off in disgust, she was startled by a familiar voice calling out, "Evening, gorgeous. I wasn't sure if I'd make it through the day without seeing your beautiful face again."

Daisy stopped and looked around. There, leaning against a lamppost and smoking a cigarette, was Derek. "I thought you weren't coming," she said.

Derek feigned surprise, "Not coming? You must be joking. A million pounds and a one-way ticket to paradise wouldn't have kept me away. So, Daisy, I've reserved the seat next to mine in the cinema this Saturday. The only question now is whether or not you'd like to occupy it."

The tension that had built up in Daisy's body subsided. She found herself staring at Derek, thinking that he looked even taller than he had earlier, and that his features were more pronounced in the daylight. Above everything else, he had a certain way about him that put her at ease.

"Yes," Daisy said, bursting with excitement. She handed over a scrap of paper with her address scribbled on it. "But I have to be home by ten o'clock sharp."

Derek blew Daisy a kiss. "I'll come to your place at six o'clock on the dot, and I'll have you back by no later than ten."

* * * *

Three days seemed more like three months to Daisy. Finally, the weekend came around. Her work finished at four o'clock on Saturdays. If she hurried, she had nearly two hours to get herself ready. The previous evening, she ironed her favorite dress; all that remained was to wash and fix her hair. After considering options, she settled on letting her brown locks flow naturally around her shoulders, hoping this would make her look a little older than her sixteen years.

By five-thirty, Daisy had her coat and handbag ready. She looked anxiously out of the living room window. The minutes passed slowly. At precisely six o'clock a black Austin Seven pulled up outside her front door with Derek at the wheel.

"He's here, Mum," she shouted. "I'll see you later. And I promise to be home by ten."

Despite the concern for her daughter's well-being, Daisy's mother put on a brave face. "Enjoy yourself." She said, knowing that her daughter was growing up and inevitably would be going out more often.

When Derek saw Daisy, he ran around and opened the passenger door. "Your carriage awaits, my princess," he said with a smile.

"Is this your car?" Daisy exclaimed.

"Of course it is," Derek said, leaving Daisy marveling at how someone of his age could possibly afford such an extravagance.

The first film was a short comedy, and though Daisy enjoyed it, she was looking forward to the main attraction. *The Flame of Love*, one of the most controversial films made in 1930, was a romance featuring John Longden and Amy May Wong, in which the co-stars would sleep together. Daisy never took her eyes off the screen and was still entranced when the audience rose up to sing, "God Save the King."

On the short drive back to Daisy's house, Derek held her hand. He parked his car and turned off the lights. "We still have twenty minutes before my carriage turns into a pumpkin," he said, putting one arm around Daisy's shoulder.

Daisy was enjoying the warmth of their closeness, and when Derek's lips found hers, she experienced a tingling sensation all down her spine. She hoped the time would pass slowly. In what seemed like a blink of the eye, Derek said, "Are you ready for your beauty sleep? Not that you need it, of course."

Daisy pressed hers lips against Derek's one last time. "Thank you for a wonderful evening. I couldn't imagine anything that I would have enjoyed more," she said, wondering what Derek's parting words might be.

"I had a great time, Daisy. Why don't we get together tomorrow? I'll take you for a spin in my jalopy, and then give you a personal tour of my castle."

Daisy laughed. "That would be smashing. Could you collect me after lunch? I'm sure mum won't mind me being out for the afternoon. I mustn't get home too late in case she needs help."

"I'll be here at one-thirty sharp," Derek said, escorting Daisy to her doorstep.

"Did you have a nice evening, love?" Daisy's mother asked. She was certain from the look on her daughter's face what the answer would be.

"Oh, Mum, it was brilliant. I really enjoyed the film. Derek is such a gentleman, and very good looking. He's taking me out tomorrow afternoon. Please don't worry. I'll be back well before you turn in for the night.

* * * *

Daisy was looking out the window when Derek drew up on the stroke of one-thirty. She kissed her mother goodbye then ran outside where Derek was holding the car door open for her. "Did you sleep well?" he asked.

"Yes, I did," Daisy replied, snuggling up close as they pulled away.

"I'm going to take you around the dockland markets and warehouses. That's where I do most of my business. Then back to my castle for a tour."

Daisy laughed. "What do you do for a living, Derek?"

"I'm a trader," he said, without elaborating. Daisy wasn't sure what he meant, and she didn't want to pry. In any event, she thought he must have an amazing job to be able to buy a car.

On their drive Derek pointed out many of the businesses and factories by name. Daisy was impressed, realizing how lucky she'd been to meet someone who was handsome, good company and clearly "a man of the world." With her thoughts focused on Derek, she was startled when the car came to a screeching halt. "Welcome to Taylor Towers," Derek said, pointing at the brown door with a silver knocker in the shape of a lion's head.

Derek's flat was larger than Daisy had imagined. Two bedrooms, a living room, a scullery, and an indoor toilet—a luxury that few people in the area enjoyed. Returning to the living room, Derek asked, "What's your poison?" pointing at the array of bottles sitting on top of the sideboard. "We must celebrate our new friendship."

Daisy's experience with alcohol was limited. She'd drunk a small mixture of lemonade and beer the previous Christmas, and her mother kept a bottle of brandy, which she sipped on if she had a chill. Wanting to appear like an adult, Daisy carefully studied the choice of drinks. She was thrilled when she recognized the one labeled Harvey's Bristol Cream. "I'll try this," she said enthusiastically.

Derek poured sherry for Daisy, whiskey for himself.

"Here's to us," he said, clinking glasses and taking a large gulp, gesturing for Daisy to do the same.

They sat on the settee, chatting and sipping on their drinks. Daisy noticed that Derek's manner had mellowed.

"You really are beautiful, Daisy," he said, kissing her lips lightly. "I'm lucky to have met you."

"Thank you, Derek. I feel the same way."

Derek smiled and refilled their glasses. Daisy had never felt this close to a man before. She was enjoying both the warmth permeating from Derek's body and the relaxing effect of the sherry.

They continued to chat idly, making eyes at each other, and kissing frequently. All the while, Derek continued to refill their glasses as they emptied. Every kiss became more passionate, and in the process, Daisy's inhibitions started to fade. When Derek squeezed her more tightly, she ran her fingers through his hair, kissed his neck and nibbled on his ear. *Love*, she thought to herself, *there couldn't possibly be anything more breathtaking.*

Daisy knew that she'd drunk more than she should have and she was beginning to feel light-headed. Regardless, she decided to follow her heart rather than her head. *What woman, snuggled up to a handsome man she was falling in love with, wouldn't?* She asked herself. Following an extended embrace, Derek gently placed one hand on Daisy's left breast. When he was sure that she was aroused by his touching, he lowered his hand and ran it along the inside of her thighs. Daisy's mind was drifting away. She no longer knew in which direction, and she didn't much care either. She only wanted to enjoy the moment.

* * * *

By the time Derek had finished rebuttoning his shirt and trousers, Daisy had fallen asleep. He poured himself another whiskey and lit a cigarette, waiting for Daisy to wake up. One hour later, she was still snoring quietly, so he pushed her gently. With no sign of movement, he shook her until she stirred. Gradually, her mind re-engaged. Her mouth felt furry and her head throbbed. Slowly, she began to recall the events that had taken place earlier, though the details remained fuzzy. When she sat up and saw that her blouse was undone and her panties were below her knees, there was no need to speculate further.

Reality set in and Daisy found herself in a state of disbelief. She didn't know what to make of it. She could hardly imagine herself being in such a position. Having sex with someone she barely knew seemed too outrageous to be true. Why, oh, why, did she have all those drinks? Surely she wouldn't have behaved the way she had without them. For a moment, she felt herself panic, as if she was in the middle of a bad dream. Then she calmed herself. What was the point of getting upset—what had happened had happened. And maybe it wasn't such a terrible thing, not if she and Derek cared deeply for each other.

When her self-confidence returned, Daisy rearranged her clothing, crossed the room and sat down on Derek's lap. "I've never felt this way before," she said, putting hers arms around Derek's shoulders and pressing her cheek against his.

"Well, I'm pleased you've woken up at last. We need to get going, or you'll be late."

"Really, what time is it?"

"It's six-thirty. I don't want your mother worrying."

"Just a few more minutes," Daisy said, embarking on another lengthy kiss.

When Daisy came up for air, Derek eased her off of his lap. "Come on, Daisy, let's go," he said tersely.

Derek's abruptness surprised Daisy. She told herself he was only acting responsibly, and avoiding any anguish on her mother's part. On the short drive back to her house, she sat with one hand on Derek's thigh and her head resting on his shoulder. The physical closeness she was enjoying ended abruptly. Derek braked hard, causing her to bounce backwards. "We've arrived," he announced in a loud voice, jumping out of the car and running around to open the passenger door.

"Couldn't we just sit here and talk for a while?" Daisy asked when Derek pulled on her arm.

"No, Daisy, you need to get indoors, and I've other things to do."

Daisy tried to give Derek a hug. He rejected her advance. "What's the matter?" she asked, her eyes filling with tears.

Derek shrugged, "Nothing," he said, walking around to the driver's door.

"When will I see you again?" Daisy cried out.

"Look, it was fun while it lasted. Let's not make it into something that it wasn't," Derek called back. He started the car's engine and accelerated away.

Daisy was numb. How could a man behave this way? Especially after demonstrating he loved her. The harsh reality set in. Heartbroken, recognizing that Derek had never shared her feelings and had only been using her, she began to cry. Not wanting her mother to see her present condition, she walked slowly around the block until she was able to regain control of her emotions. She told her mother she had a headache and would be going straight to bed. She knew she wouldn't be able to spend the rest of the evening pretending nothing was wrong.

For the first time since her father's death, Daisy cried herself to sleep.

* * * *

In keeping with Derek Taylor's mindset, his fling with Daisy was quickly forgotten. He got mileage from bragging to his mates that he'd scored with a young virgin; now he was exploring new pastures. Expecting a friend to visit, he was completely taken aback when he answered a knock on his front door one Sunday morning to find Daisy standing there. "We need to talk. Can I come inside?"

Momentarily flustered, he showed her into the living room where they stared at each other in silence. "I'm pregnant!" she finally blurted out, holding her stomach with outstretched fingers to help illustrate her condition.

Derek was agape. He'd never faced a situation like this. He didn't like being confronted, so he became defiant.

"Why are you telling me?" he snapped back.

"You're asking me why? What's the matter with you? You're the father. Why else would I be telling you?"

Derek smirked. "I don't think you can prove that."

Normally mild mannered, Daisy was infuriated by Derek's words and attitude. "You bastard!" she screamed, slapping his face so hard her fingers tingled. "You're the only boy who's ever touched me. You brought about this situation. Now I'm expecting you to do the honorable thing."

"And what might that be?" he asked, lightly touching the five red stripes that were stinging his left cheek.

"I'm expecting you to marry me of course; what else could you possibly think?"

"Sorry, darling, that's not going to happen," Derek said, regaining his composure and grinning again.

"We'll see about that. You might not know right from wrong, but your mother does!" Daisy replied, glaring with anger.

Derek's expression instantly changed, taking on the look of a boxer who hadn't seen the last punch coming. "What's my mother got to do with it?" he asked timidly. She was the only woman he had ever listened to.

"Plenty, as it so happens. You see my mum goes to St. Francis church on Sundays if she's feeling well. She told the vicar about my situation, and it turns out he's very close with your mother, who, by the way, will be paying you a visit later today."

Derek's face turned chalk white, and for once, he was speechless.

* * * *

Derek Taylor had talked himself out of many predicaments in his short life. He hadn't managed a repeat performance before he and Daisy were married at the local registrar office. Their mothers witnessed the short ceremony, and afterward, they returned to Derek's family home, where they were joined by his sisters for tea and cake.

It had been a major embarrassment for Daisy to explain to her mother what had happened. To her surprise and relief, she had taken it quite well. "You've been very silly, my dear, but we all make mistakes. You have to make the most of them. Hopefully, Derek will turn out to be a good husband and father in the long run."

Daisy knew that marrying Derek had its risks. Despite this, she decided the possibility of building a united family was preferable to going it alone. In any event, how would she be able to raise a child without working? And giving her baby up for adoption was unthinkable.

Following the wedding, Daisy moved in with Derek, determined to make a go of it. Each morning she got up early to visit and check on her mother and again on her way home. Then she spent the evenings cooking and cleaning, trying to create a comfortable atmosphere. At first, Derek appeared receptive to a calmer and more orderly existence. That didn't last for long. As the weeks ticked by, both his drinking and mood swings increased significantly. Daisy threw away many uneaten meals she'd spent hours preparing.

Prior to their marriage, Daisy had understood Derek to be a trader. When a pattern emerged with unsavory characters dropping off boxes late at night, it gradually dawned on her how Derek really made his living.

* * * *

In the late afternoon of June 5th, 1931, Daisy gave birth to a six-pound baby boy. She had tried to discuss possible names for their child with Derek. To her dismay the only response she got was, "I don't give a damn." She decided to name the baby Alan, in memory of her late father.

* * * *

Back on her feet, Daisy did her best to care for Alan. At the same time, dealing with Derek's increasingly uncompromising behavior was taking its toll. Daisy's patience reached a new low, and she began drinking the odd nip of gin after putting Alan down for his nap. This habit quickly got worse. Within weeks, she was drinking two or three large glasses each day. The resulting hangovers only added to her misery.

Knowing her life was spinning out of control, Daisy attempted a desperate last ditch effort to reason with her husband. "Derek, we have to talk. We both know things aren't what they should be. We need to put that aside and think about young Alan and his future."

"All right, Daisy," he said, cutting her off. "Look, I've got a busy and important day ahead of me. Let's talk tonight."

That evening, Daisy fed Alan and put him down for the night. She waited patiently for Derek to get home. At eleven o'clock, he still hadn't arrived. She went to bed frustrated; still determined to have her heart-to-heart with Derek the following morning. She was just dozing off when she heard the front door open, and what sounded like two men whispering. She got out of bed, put on her dressing gown, and tip toed along the hallway to investigate. Peeking around the doorway, she saw two of Derek's associates. They were opening the boxes that had been delivered the previous evening and stuffing their contents into a battered brown suitcase.

"What are you doing in my home?" she screamed. "And where's Derek?"

"Sorry, Daisy," Charlie said softly, "We were trying to be quiet. We didn't want to wake you or the baby."

"That doesn't answer my question, and how did you get in here anyway?"

Charlie held up a key, "Derek gave us this and asked us to pick up some of his gear."

"What are you talking about? And I'll ask just one more time. Where is Derek?"

"Look, we had some business earlier this evening. It was all going smoothly until, out of the blue, a security guard showed. Apparently, he was a last-minute replacement for the one Derek thought he'd already paid off. Well, let's just say that he wasn't very friendly, so we had no choice."

"No choice over what?" Daisy asked, beginning to tremble.

"We had to take care of him. We didn't mean him any real harm, but the silly sod kept on fighting. Finally, we tossed him down the stairs. We thought that would shut him up long enough for us all to get away. We didn't anticipate that he would roll over and land smack on top of his head."

Daisy flinched. "How bad was it, Charlie?" not sure if she really wanted to get an answer.

"We didn't stop to find out. Derek had some other business to take care of. We're meeting him later at the train station. Then we're going up north until this all blows over."

Daisy's body froze as she mumbled, "When will I see Derek again?"

Charlie ignored her question. "We must run, Daisy. Before I leave, there's something that Derek asked me to give you." He opened his wallet and handed over twenty pounds.

*   *   *   *

Following Derek's disappearance, Daisy faced a two edged dilemma. On the one hand, she didn't want to go out in case she bumped into someone who knew her situation. On the other hand, she was petrified that the police may call while she was home. To avoid contact with others, she made brief early morning visits to check on her mother and ran to the shops to buy essentials during off-peak hours. Daisy's feeling of helplessness continued to grow daily. She knew it was impossible to hide indefinitely, and in any event, the money Derek had left wouldn't last forever.

Alan had just gone down for his afternoon nap when Daisy heard a knock on the front door. Certain it was the police, she hid behind the settee until it occurred to her they'd break in if she didn't answer. Daisy felt faint and unsteady on her feet. She fumbled to open the door— only to find a neighbor standing there. "Hello, Brenda," she whispered. "Can I help you?"

"I haven't seen you around, Daisy. I thought I'd stop by to see if everything's all right."

Daisy hoped Brenda wouldn't notice her hands shaking. "Yes, thank you," were the only words she could manage.

Brenda looked more closely at her neighbor. "Daisy, I know it's none of my business. Are you sure everything's all right?" Daisy didn't know how to respond. Contact with another person was making her uncomfortable, but she didn't want to appear rude or ungrateful. She hesitated before deciding to invite Brenda inside. When the door closed behind her, Daisy started weeping, and after settling herself, she told Brenda the whole story.

"You poor thing, what are you going to do now?" Brenda asked.

"I've no idea," She said, fighting back tears. "My mother can't support us, and I don't know if we'll ever get help from Derek. I've got to do something. In all honesty I don't have a clue. I'd rather kill myself than give Alan up for adoption."

Brenda had been touched by what she'd heard earlier. Daisy's last remark hit a really raw nerve. "Can you keep a secret?"

"I promise," Daisy replied softly.

Brenda paused to gather her thoughts. "We have more in common than you may think. When I was seventeen, I fell in love with a young man. My parents didn't approve, but I ignored them. He wanted to sleep with me. I told him we needed to wait until we were married." Brenda bit her lip. "I loved him so much Daisy. I would have done anything to keep him, so I gave him what he wanted." She laughed bitterly. "Sure enough, six weeks later, a baby was on the way. He'd always told me how much he loved me, so I thought he'd be pleased." Her voice dropped to a whisper, "But when I gave him the news he screamed obscenities and punched me in the face."

Daisy cupped her cheeks with her hands and gasped. "Good grief. Were you injured?"

"A black eye and a cut lip. Physical wounds heal. Memories, however, stay forever." Brenda's head dropped slightly, and her eyes started to well up. "Talking of memories, he also left me with a souvenir. I suppose I shouldn't have been surprised that the stupid piece of shit couldn't even spell."

Brenda lifted her skirt to reveal an uneven scar in the shape of the letter H. "Apparently, he thought this would permanently brand me as a whore."

Daisy was horrified. She felt sick imagining a man intentionally burning his girlfriend's leg.

"I thought things couldn't get any worse. I was wrong. My parents were unsympathetic. They threw me out of the house, saying I was a good for nothing slut. Luckily, my aunt put me up until the baby was born. When

I stopped working she couldn't afford to keep me, let alone my daughter."

"What did you do?" Daisy asked, noticing the tear drops sliding down Brenda's cheeks.

"I was at my wit's end. Out of desperation, I did something I never dreamed myself capable of."

Daisy waited for Brenda to elaborate.

"My elderly aunt was only able to care for my daughter for a few hours each day. Part-time work didn't pay enough for me to get by. That is, until I came across an unlikely opportunity." Brenda cleared her throat, "I became a stripper at the Sunlight Club."

Daisy tried to hide her shock. She knew her neighbor had just bared her soul.

"I got lucky. I'd only been stripping for a few months when I met Donald. He was a lot older than me, and I suppose, if I'm honest, the relationship wouldn't have gone far in different circumstances. Fortunately, he happily accepted my daughter along with me. We got married and he still treats both of us extremely well. I have a lot to be grateful for."

The two women sat quietly, reflecting on the past. Daisy broke the silence. "Do you mind if I ask a personal question?"

"Go ahead," Brenda responded, trying to force a smile.

"What's it like being a stripper?"

Brenda pulled a face. "It's hard to find the right words. I doubt there are many things in this life that could possibly be more embarrassing and degrading. Like the other girls, I found ways to cope. I always had a tipple or two prior to going on stage. I also got some comfort from the wig and heavy makeup I wore, because I thought they helped to disguise me."

"I suppose I've never really thought about it. Aren't strip clubs against the law?"

"Of course they are. But Daisy, you know how things work around these parts. The manager is a close friend of the police sergeant, and the club engages off-duty officers as bouncers. It's the same old thing. It's not what you know, rather, who you know."

"Did you have to audition?" Daisy asked, curiosity getting the better of her.

Brenda frowned, "I wouldn't exactly call it an audition. I was invited into the manager's office, expecting to answer a few questions. I could tell that he was a dirty old sod. I didn't anticipate him being so blunt. He sat in his chair, lit his pipe, and asked me to show him all that I'd got."

Daisy was wide-eyed. "Did he mean that literally?" she asked.

"He most certainly did. He just gawked at me until finally my panties were around my ankles. Then he looked me up and down a couple of times and said, 'You'll do Brenda, you can start next Monday.' I suppose if nothing else, stripping in front of that pervert was a good indication of what lay ahead."

Emboldened by Brenda's frankness, Daisy asked, "Well, obviously you had what the manager was looking for. Purely out of interest, do you think he'd find me suitable?"

Brenda looked Daisy over and a cheeky grin appeared on her face. "Sweetheart, take a look at yourself in the mirror when you undress for bed this evening. Then I think you'll be able to answer your own question."

Daisy was flattered by Brenda's compliment, and when she opened the door to say goodbye to her neighbor, she felt more at ease than she had an hour earlier. In spite of her improved mood, she knew her circumstances remained unchanged. She tried to rationalize the situation and her next move. One thing was for certain—she would do anything to avoid parting with Alan. What were her options? Perhaps, there was only one. She cringed.

CHAPTER

George Lambert and his sister were playing cards in the upstairs bedroom. They heard the front door open, and seconds later, their mother let out a blood curdling scream. Seeing the fear in his sibling's eyes, young George told his sister to hide under the bed while he went downstairs to investigate. Dreading what may have happened, and sensing the intruder was still in the house, he braced himself. If someone was hurting his mother, he would defend her at any cost. Approaching the living room, he noticed a broom balanced against the wall. He grabbed it, ready to attack.

Summoning up all the strength he could muster, George charged through the door, where to his amazement he saw his mother kissing a man dressed in a soldier's uniform.

"Hello son. My, how you've grown," the soldier said, turning around to face George.

George stopped dead in his tracks. "Sheila, Sheila, come quickly! Dad's back," he shouted at the top of his lungs.

*   *   *   *

James Lambert was a labor foreman. In 1914, he was called to serve in World War I. He prayed he would make it through in one piece, knowing the terrible burden it would put on his wife if she were forced to raise two young children alone. Fortunately, James survived the horrors of trench warfare, and his appreciation and devotion to family reached a new high upon his safe return.

"What do you think young George wants to do when his school days are over?" James asked his wife one evening after their children were tucked in for the night.

"I'm surprised you even ask. Surely, you must know by now that your son worships the ground you walk on. He only wants to follow in your footsteps."

James glowed with pride. "In that case, I'll get him started this coming weekend. It will be good for him to learn how things work at the market."

At four o'clock on Saturday morning, James Lambert prodded his son. "It's time to get up. We need to leave in thirty minutes."

The two of them devoured porridge, gulped down hot tea, and then set off on their fifteen-minute walk to the market. There, George helped the gang his father supervised set up stands, stack boxes, and if necessary, act as a runner—something he would do every Saturday for the next two years.

The fact that James Lambert was a foreman didn't stop the labor gang from playing practical jokes on George. It was a long-standing tradition. George never complained and took the men's actions in his stride, often laughing along with them if made to look foolish.

With work over, George walked contentedly alongside his father on their journey home. He always enjoyed the day and knew still further rewards awaited him. When they reached their two-up-two-down terraced house, his sister would fuss over him while his mother prepared a hot supper. The experience George gained at the market gave him a sense of purpose, and the pride he felt watching his father direct the crew left him in no doubt where he'd work when school was over.

* * * *

In August 1920, George signed up to become a laborer at Northgate market. Originally, it had been a small lot where local growers met to exchange or sell produce. Now, it covered five acres and sold a variety of goods from all over the region.

George couldn't wait to get to work each day. He thrived on the market's ever-changing tapestry and the camaraderie he shared with co-workers. There were always new smells, sounds, and interesting people to meet: farmers, many whom spoke with thick colloquial accents, gypsies dressed in brightly-colored clothes, selling candles and woven baskets, and other salesmen whose products ranged from fragrant perfumes to obnoxious chemicals. These aromas were laced with the ever-present smell of horse manure, together with the pungent odor of gasoline fumes belching from truck exhausts.

It didn't take long for George's workmates to discover his talent for mending things. When this came to the manager's attention, he was often asked to fix boxes and pieces of equipment that were damaged or broken during daily use. If necessary, this was done in his own time, which gained the respect of co-workers and made his father proud.

Second in line to the manager was the timekeeper. All employees had to check in with him each morning, and he had the authority to deduct wages in the event of late arrival. He was also responsible for blowing the horn, indicating the end of a work day. Prior to the war, this resulted in an immediate exodus. In recent years, a new tradition had started. On hearing the finish signal, the workers ran to the timekeeper's hut. Once assembled, they began hurling abusive or irreverent remarks.

"Late with the horn again!" one would shout.

"He wouldn't know. His bloody watch stopped weeks ago!" another would scream.

"Even if it hadn't, it wouldn't help, cos he can't tell the fucking time!" another yelled.

"Tell the time? He couldn't tell you the day of the week!"

"Year, more like it," another added.

"You have to feel sorry for the poor old sod. At his age, it's surprising he still gets up each morning."

"I heard his wife tell someone he hasn't got it up in years," a voice from the back called out. Along with the shrieking and hollering, this remark brought obscene gestures, inferring the timekeeper's impotence.

When the boys finished laughing, the timekeeper put his hands on his hips and scanned those around him with a scowl on his face. "Listen to me, you scruffy bunch of bastards. Even if you're only the width of a gnat's cock late, I'll still dock you an hour. Now piss off home you good-for-nothing louts, or you'll find my boot up your backside."

As he spat out the words, the veins in his neck protruded and his cheeks turned crimson. This was pure theater for members of the public looking on. All the workers knew it was only a charade. George looked forward to this daily event; he found it amusing and uplifting. Occasionally, he chimed in with a witty quip or two of his own, though like his father, he seldom used profanity. He asked his dad on one occasion how this tradition started.

"It beats me, George. The timekeeper hardly spoke to anyone before the war. Back then, if one of the workers talked to him like they do today, he'd probably knock their front teeth out."

The timekeeper was a tough old bugger. He'd worked full-time at the market since age twelve and had long been known only by his nickname, Slugger. He'd been an accomplished boxer in his youth, and even now in his early sixties, he still struck an imposing figure. Early in his career, he kept himself to himself. More recently, his personality had softened considerably. In 1914, his only son was called into duty, and the following year, he perished on the Western Front. Slugger had never mentioned his son since the day a brown envelope from the government arrived. To the world at large he remained stoic. Only his wife knew the man everyone considered fearless had a broken heart that would never mend. She was also certain the only thing that kept it ticking was his daily roasting from the boys.

* * * *

In 1924, George turned eighteen. Now, he was established at the market and beginning to feel like a man. Not yet on a par with his dear dad, but well on his way. He knew he was lucky to be part of a close and loving family. He worked with several boys who were not so fortunate. He wondered if he would have a family of his own one day. He certainly hoped so.

* * * *

On a chilly morning in June 1925, George first set eyes on Lilly. He was passing a florist's stall located near the market entrance, where he spotted her arranging fresh flowers. He found himself attracted by her sparkling green eyes and her long, dark hair flowing with the breeze. His experience with girls was limited. He occasionally mixed with some of his sister's friends, but he'd never been on a date. He hoped Lilly would notice him walking slowly past her stall. To his chagrin, she didn't. In an effort to improve his odds, the next morning he whistled loudly while passing and this did the trick. When their eyes met, George said, "Good morning," a greeting that Lilly returned. Though George found this encouraging, he couldn't think how best to take the next step. He shared this dilemma with his sister.

"First of all, you have to get to know her. Don't rush or push, and try not to rehearse a speech. If you do, it most likely will put her off. Just act naturally. If she's interested, you'll soon find out."

Later in the week, George plucked up courage and stopped in front of the florist's stall. "Good morning, Miss. I'm George. I've seen you several times recently, and I was wondering what name would match such a pretty face?" He tried to remain calm, hoping she wouldn't notice the beads of sweat forming on his forehead. The young girl blushed. "Nice to meet you as well, George. My name's Lilly."

"An appropriate name, if I may say so," he said, looking at the flowers she was holding, "Funny, because I had a feeling it might be Rose or Violet."

Lilly chuckled. She'd come to appreciate the market humor.

"How long have you worked here?"

"Only two months. My first job was polishing shoes. I was fortunate enough to get this job a year later. I much prefer to work in the fresh air, and I love having the smell of flowers surround me all day long."

"You're lucky. I wouldn't tell a young lady about some of the smells I have to put up with. And I'm not only referring to the goods we handle."

Lilly tittered, catching the innuendo, but also the attention of the stall supervisor.

"I hope your job isn't interfering with your personal life, young lady!" she called out sarcastically.

Lilly rolled her eyes at George, and when the supervisor turned away, he pushed his nose up with his thumb. Lilly suppressed the urge to laugh, knowing it may get her into trouble.

"Must dash, Lilly, or I'll be late." He lowered his voice to a whisper. "If I don't leave soon, I fancy we'll both be looking for another job."

Every subsequent morning George greeted Lilly and they regularly exchanged polite words. While he wanted the relationship to grow quickly, he heeded his sister's advice. He waited patiently for a month before deciding it was time to take another step.

The following morning, he felt on top of the world. The feeling didn't last for long. When the flower stall came into sight, his confidence waned considerably. He stopped for a moment and took several deep breathes. He hoped it would relieve the knot that had started in his stomach and now risen up to his throat.

Unbeknownst to George, Lilly was watching, suspecting his actions were leading to some kind of prank. Not wanting to spoil the fun, she pretended not to notice him until he stopped opposite her stall. If George had been making a stage debut at a West End theater, Lilly would have immediately diagnosed his condition. She assumed that standing silently was part of the act—until she noticed he was trembling.

"Are you all right George?" she asked.

Realizing that he'd blown his chances, he just gazed at Lilly and said haplessly, "Yes, thank you. I was going to ask something. I don't think it matters now."

"What were you going to ask?"

George looked vacant and he remained silent, prompting Lilly to repeat her question. Weakly, he replied, "I was going to ask if I could take you out next Sunday."

A bemused look spread over Lilly's face, which George interpreted as the precursor to a rejection. To his surprise and delight, the expression changed to a sweet smile. "I'd love that, George. What time would you like to get together?"

* * * *

George counted the days leading up to the weekend. On Saturday afternoon, he polished his leather boots and his mother pressed a Sunday best shirt. Knowing the date was important his father let George borrow a checkered waist coat and matching cloth cap. At eight o'clock on Sunday morning, his mother gave him a hug.

"Good luck, son. Today reminds me of my first outing with your dad. Remember your manners and always listen to what Lilly has to say. It's a sign of respect—something many girls feel they don't get enough of. Don't try too hard to impress her. She'll get to know you soon enough, and then she'll be sure you're a good 'un. No need to be a comedian, but nearly all girls like a laugh."

"Thank you, Mum. I'm so nervous. I'm just hoping I don't make a fool of myself."

"You'll do just fine. Now be off with you."

Lilly's house was only a ten-minute walk, but being late was out of the question. Arriving with twenty minutes to spare, George hung around opposite the house until his pocket watch indicated it was eight-twenty-nine. He crossed the road, walked up to number 62, and, using the large black door knocker, banged twice. A few seconds later the door opened, revealing a bald-headed man several inches shorter than himself.

"I suppose you're here to see my daughter," the man said gruffly, looking George up and down. "Well, if nothing else, at least it looks like you've washed," he added, turning around and shouting down the hallway. "Lilly, he's here!"

"Thank you," George said to the man who was already disappearing through a doorway. Moments later, Lilly appeared. She was wearing a blue dress and her shiny dark hair flowed gently around her shoulders. George was hypnotized. He'd always found her attractive, even though the long green apron and white bonnet she wore at the stall weren't flattering. Now she looked positively beautiful.

*   *   *   *

The young couple had been dating for four months. One weekend, they went to watch Charlie Chaplin starring in *The Kid* and that evening, George told Lilly for the first time that he loved her. Two months later, on a rainy Saturday afternoon, they took early tea at a café close to

Tower Bridge. It was still drizzling when they left, but being a warm evening, they decided to walk home. Half-way across the bridge, George stopped and bent down on one knee, "Would you do me the honor of giving me your hand in marriage, my darling?" he asked, gazing into the eyes of the young woman he'd grown to adore.

Lilly gasped and let out a shriek of delight, "Yes, George. Yes, I will."

Despite only knowing George for a little more than six months, Lilly had no doubts. In addition to finding George handsome, she knew he was kind, thoughtful, and courteous—a perfect partner for the life she'd dreamed about.

Seven months later, the happy couple married at a small church in East London before moving in with Lilly's parents.

* * * *

Lilly's father had a cousin, Henry Wilson, who'd relocated to Essex a few years earlier to open a car repair and maintenance business. Henry and his wife spoke with Lilly's father at the wedding reception, who told them that George was an especially nice and talented young man. "Clever with his hands, I'm told. I wouldn't be surprised if he does really well if he gets half a chance."

He'd forgotten the conversation with his cousin, but was reminded upon opening a letter from him two weeks later. Having read the content, he asked the family to assemble around the kitchen table.

"I've just heard from my cousin, Henry," Lilly's father started out. "Let me read you his letter.

Dear Cousin,

Susan and I enjoyed the wedding and reception for Lilly and her new husband. They make a nice couple, and I'm sure they'll be happy together. You mentioned George was clever with his hands and I thought about your remark when we arrived back home. The business is going well, but I have a problem keeping mechanics. I'm sure you know, more and more people are buying cars, so new repair shops keep opening. To get started they often offer higher wages. As a result, I keep losing employees. If George has the aptitude to mend things, I'm sure I could train him to do the work needed. It would be wonderful to have family members in the firm. I think I could pay George more than he makes at the market, and there'd be a spot for Lilly because Susan would like to spend less time working in the office. Above our workshop is an area that could easily be converted into living space, so they wouldn't have to worry about finding a home. I'm hoping you will discuss this with them, and if they have any interest, perhaps you would let me know. I'd be happy to drive up and talk with them whenever it's convenient.

Your cousin, Henry.

Lilly's father looked around the table, waiting for a reaction. His wife was the first to speak. "It's hard to imagine not having our Lilly around. I'm sure George's parents will feel the same way. But it does sound like a chance for the two of them to get ahead. How long does it take to get to Essex anyway?" she asked, looking at her husband.

"According to Henry, it's about an hour by car. Not sure how long if you take a train, as I've never done it," he replied.

"So, what do you two think?" Lilly's mother asked, looking at George and her daughter. Lilly turned to her husband, gesturing for him respond.

"I must say, this all comes as a surprise. We need to give it some thought. Then we can talk further." George looked at Lilly to see if she had anything to add. She remained silent.

"Well, that's it, then," Lilly's father concluded. "When the two of you have talked it through, let me know whether or not you're interested."

That evening, George and Lilly went to bed earlier than usual. Lilly whispered in her husband's ear. "That's a turn up for the books. I didn't see it coming, did you?"

"No, I didn't. I barely spoke to Henry or his wife at the reception, and we certainly didn't talk about his business."

"Being away from family would be hard. I must say that having our own place and making a bit more money sounds quite appealing. What about you?" Lilly asked.

"I agree it offers some advantages. I'm concerned about the job. I may be able to fix boxes and replace barrow wheels, but I don't know the first thing about cars."

Lilly squeezed her husband tightly. "George Lambert, you can do anything if you put your mind to it. Let's sleep on it, and by the way, I want you to make the final decision."

"Why do you say that? Surely it should be both of us?"

"George, love, I'd be happy living on the moon if I was with you. Whatever you choose, I'll gladly support." Lilly sighed contentedly, falling asleep in her husband's arms.

The following evening, the newlyweds took off for a walk. "I've had Henry's letter on my mind since the moment we woke up," George told his wife. "You know, this might be a good opportunity, but it's also a big move. We need to be careful and make sure we know what we'd be letting ourselves in for. I think we should meet Henry to run over the details. Then chew on it before making up our minds."

"Good idea, George. Remember what I told you last night; I'm going to leave the decision to you."

George kissed his wife. "Well, let's go and tell your parents what we'd like to do next."

* * * *

Henry planned his journey to arrive at the Pig and Whistle pub shortly after opening time. Spotting George sitting in the far corner, he shouted out, "Is it a pint of bitter?"

George looked up. "Hello, Henry, just a half for me, thanks," he said, trying to picture life in Essex.

Henry brought the drinks to the table where George was sitting alone. "How's married life treating you?" he asked, taking a large swig of his beer.

"I couldn't imagine it being any better. I'm so lucky to have Lilly."

"She always was a lovely girl. Of course, you'd be asking the wrong person. I'd agree you were lucky."

The two men laughed and then Henry took on a more serious manner. "Well, George, let's get down to business. I know my cousin told you what I'm interested in. So, what do you think?"

"It sounds good, but we have a number of questions. First off, I'd like to know more about the job. To be honest, Henry, I really don't know much about cars. I also need to make sure Lilly's comfortable. You know her, she's very accommodating. I want to be certain she's happy with the living arrangements, and whatever jobs you need her to do. Then there's the matter of family. Lilly will be upset if she can't see her parents from time to time. Do you have any ideas?"

"I'm pleased you've given it some thought. I know it's a big move, and if you decide to go ahead, I'm as keen as you are that it all works out. My cousin would kill me if I upset his daughter. With regard to the work, I have no worries. I learned from scratch, and it's just a matter of practice if you've got the knack for mending things. I'll start you off on routine jobs like changing tires and oil, then, you can watch and learn from me. I've also got a book that could help."

Henry took another swig of his beer. "With regard to Lilly, she's a bright girl. Susan will teach her to type and file in no time. Our workshop was used for manufacturing before we bought it. Upstairs are rooms where the young workers lived. It does need some improvements. I know a builder who can take care of that. It has two bedrooms, so family could visit.

Henry scratched his head. "Talking of visiting, I've got a motorbike you can borrow whenever you like, and I'll soon teach you to ride it. I know family is important. I'd be prepared to let you take one Saturday off every two months. That reminds me of something. I took the liberty of asking my cousin about your wages. I'd be happy to match them for the first six months while you're learning. Assuming everything works out, I'll give you half as much again after that. I can also afford to match Lilly's wages. When she picks it all up, I'm betting she'd be done in five or six hours each day. That will give her the chance to take care of housework, so the two of you can have evenings to yourselves."

George had intended to mull things over, but the opportunity Henry outlined was better than he could have possibly imagined. He got to his feet and took Henry's hand, "You've got a deal, and I promise we won't let you down."

* * * *

On the morning of their departure, George visited his parents' home to say farewell. "Take good care, George, my darling," his mother said, her eyes filling with tears.

"I will, Mum. And please don't worry. We'll visit every two months, I promise."

James Lambert looked his offspring squarely in the eye. "I'm proud of you, son. Just remember, always look out for Lilly."

"Rest assured, Dad. I will. And thanks for all you've done."

George's sister, Sheila, didn't say a word. She didn't need to. Her looks and demeanor told its own story. She hugged her brother tightly and kissed him on the cheek. Separating from his sibling was equally painful for George. The bond between brother and sister had grown strong over the years.

Lilly had promised herself not to cry. When she heard Henry's car pull up outside, she could no longer contain herself. George shook Lilly's father's hand, promising to take good care of his daughter. Lilly and her mother hugged and cried together, until their tears were replaced with smiles. "I'll drop you a line as soon as we get settled, Mum," were Lilly's parting words.

* * * *

After getting past a few anxious nights, the Lambert's soon adapted to their new environment. George arose early each morning and had already studied the vehicles due for repair by the time Henry and the other mechanics arrived. He watched them carefully apply their trade, asking questions where appropriate. In the evenings he read the book Henry gave him, and in a matter of weeks, he was able to take on small tasks without supervision.

This didn't go unnoticed by Henry. When the six months were up, he increased George's wages as promised.

Lilly enthusiastically embraced the role of office assistant. It provided her an opportunity to learn new skills and support her husband. Henry had been correct in predicting she would pick things up quickly. Within weeks, she mastered the basic duties, and then she took over the role of cashier, preparing invoices and collecting payments.

By the end of their first year, George was on a par with the other mechanics and Lilly had the office running efficiently. George learned to ride Henry's motorcycle, allowing him and his wife to spend a weekend visiting family every two months. Everything was going exactly as planned. George and Lilly were enjoying their new lifestyle, and Henry was delighted to have a reliable mechanic that helped his business flourish.

* * * *

The Lamberts had been living in Essex for three years and continued to visit their families on a regular basis. Now, they travelled in Henry's second car which George had learned to drive. Henry increased their wages annually. This enabled them to make small improvements to their apartment, take trips to the seaside, and also put aside a little money—something George had never dreamed they'd be able to do at this stage of their lives.

One morning in early spring, George woke to find his wife vomiting in the bathroom. He was concerned because he'd never known her to be sick. She assured him it was nothing to be worried about, likely a result of something she ate the previous day. Two days later, it happened again. "I'm getting worried about you, darling."

"I'm sure it's not serious—maybe the pollen at this time of the year. Remember, we're city people, not used to living near so many trees."

"You may be right, love, but there's no point in taking chances. I want you to visit the doctor and get yourself checked."

"But George—"

"No buts about it," George interjected, waggling his forefinger. "I want you go there as soon as possible."

Lilly knew George to be a gentle person; at the same time capable of putting his foot down on matters he considered important. "I promise," Lilly told her husband with a smile.

One afternoon, later in the week, Lilly visited the workshop area. Getting George alone, she whispered in his ear. "I'm off to see Dr. Jenkins. I'll be back in time to make dinner. And by the way, I have a surprise for you tonight."

Entering their flat at six o'clock, George was immediately struck by the smell of fish wafting from the kitchen. He suspected Lilly had splashed out and purchased Dover sole; a rare treat because of the expense. More importantly, he was anxious to hear the outcome of his wife's appointment with the doctor.

Moments later, Lilly appeared carrying two plates—each one laden with Dover sole, mounds of mashed potatoes, and runner beans. Feasting his eyes on Lilly's surprise, George kissed his wife then sat down to tuck into his meal. He noticed that his wife seemed to be in a particularly good mood. This helped him relax, sure that her sickness must have been just a minor ailment. "How did things go with Dr. Jenkins?" he asked, slicing off another piece of fish.

"There's nothing for you to worry about. I do have a condition, but it won't last forever."

George look puzzled. "Sorry, darling, I'm not sure if I understand?"

Lilly reached over the dining table and took hold of her husband's hands. She looked dreamily into his eyes. "In six months from now, you're going to be a daddy," she said.

George's knife and fork dropped to the floor. He didn't notice.

CHAPTER 4

In spite of being forewarned, Daisy was still unprepared for her interview at the Sunlight Club. Even the long, hot bath she took on her arrival back home did nothing to cleanse her shame and humiliation. She was dreading starting work the following Saturday. At the same time, she knew that for Alan's sake she had to be selfless and brave.

With the interview over, Daisy agonized over how to explain the situation to her mother. She concluded that the truth would be too painful, especially in her mother's fragile state.

"Look, Mum, several things have happened recently. I hope they don't shock you." Daisy stopped to organize her thoughts. "Derek and I have not been getting along very well, and, now he's left. I don't expect him to return, and all things considered, I think we're better off without him. Naturally, Alan is too young to understand. When he's old enough, I'll tell him that his father was killed in an accident." Daisy paused, "I hope you will be able to stick with this story, Mum. I know you never like to tell lies. Under the circumstances, I think this is for the best."

Daisy's mother nodded. "I understand, dear. How will you manage now?"

"If it's all right with you, I'd like to move back into my old bedroom. There's plenty of room for Alan's cot. I've found a part-time job. It's only two or three hours a day. I'm hoping you will be able to keep an eye on Alan while I'm away. It pays enough for me to be self-sufficient, and I might even be able to help you out a bit as well."

"I'm sorry things haven't worked out for you. To be perfectly honest, I never did care much for Derek. You know that you're always welcome here—after all, it's your home. And of course I'll be able to cope with Alan for a couple of hours each day. What type of work will you be doing?"

Daisy swallowed hard. "Packing goods at a factory down in the Docklands," she said, hoping her face wasn't turning red.

* * * *

Alan Taylor stood in the corner facing the wall. His teeth were clenched and the anger inside him was making his body quiver. In the three days since starting school, he'd already learned that bad behavior was not tolerated. To make matters worse, he was sure that the boys who'd watched the teacher haul him from his chair, were secretly laughing at him.

Following Alan's first classroom humiliation, he avoided conversations with fellow students whenever possible. He feared that they might make fun of him. His next major embarrassment, however, didn't take place at school. On his walk home one afternoon, he saw two older boys from his neighborhood approaching. The taller of the two stepped in his path. "This is Daisy Taylor's son," he said to his friend, turning to Alan and sneering. "So, how's your mother?"

Intimidated by the boy's physical size and aggressive nature, Alan looked down at his shoes, "She's fine," he said in a shaky voice.

The boy sniggered. "My uncle saw her take all her clothes off at a club in the Docklands. He told me she's got big tits." The boy stared at Alan, who was visibly shuddering, his face turning red. "Sounds like your mum enjoys' dancing naked in front of men." And the two boys began to chant, "Alan's mum has big tits; Alan's mum has big tits."

Having had their fun, the boys stood aside. They continued mocking Alan until he disappeared from sight. Angry tears pricked his eyes, and the words he had just heard made him sick to his stomach. On the remainder of his journey home, his anger and frustration increased. He wished there was a way he could run back and punish the two boys. He wasn't quite certain why they'd made comments about his mother, or exactly what they meant. Somewhere in his mind, he felt she was partly to blame for what had just happened to him.

* * * *

Following a miserable and often isolated first year at school, Alan's second year brought some changes. With a new first form arriving, he began to find children whom he could influence or intimidate. He used this platform to develop more skills.

At age seven, Alan moved from the infant school to the adjoining primary school. By now, he was taller than most boys of his age and had a muscular frame, traits inherited from his father. Participating in games, particularly football, he became increasingly aware of his physical attributes. At first he hoped these would improve his popularity. Over time, he recognized they could also be put to other uses.

In the next school year, he overheard a playground conversation between two new students. At its conclusion, one boy traded a bag of marbles for a three penny piece. Alan waited for an opportunity to get the boy who'd paid for the marbles alone. On doing so, he glared down at him, asking, "Where did you get the money from?"

The fresh-faced boy shivered and said in a high-pitched voice, "My dad gives me pocket money."

"How much do you get?" Alan asked, moving in closer.

"I get sixpence a week."

"From now on, you will give me half. Every Monday at morning break time, I'll wait behind the shed. If you fail to show up or tell anyone, I'll break your fucking arm." To reinforce his point, Alan grabbed the young boy's hand and twisted it until he winced. "Next Monday," Alan repeated, pressing his forefinger into the boy's chest.

With the summer holidays approaching, Alan joined in a lunch-break football game. Racing toward the goal in possession of the ball, he was accidentally tripped by Paul Thompson. Jumping back onto his feet, he grabbed Thompson by the shoulders and screamed obscenities in his face. He hadn't expected retaliation from a boy much smaller than himself. To his surprise, Paul grabbed him around the waist and they both tumbled to the ground. Given Alan's superior strength, Paul would have taken a beating but for the fact the break duty teacher happened to be nearby. He stood them up, grabbed each one by an ear, and marched them off to the headmaster's study.

Thompson was taken in first and reappeared minutes later with tears streaming from his eyes. Next, it was Alan's turn. The headmaster admonished him then administered four healthy strokes on his rear end with a bamboo cane. Despite the pain, Alan managed to appear indifferent. Annoyed by his pupil's display of defiance, the headmaster put one hand on Alan's shoulder. Then he bent down until their noses nearly touched. "Listen up, Taylor. If you disrespect me again, you'll live to regret it. Fighting is not tolerated at this school, and I trust I'll never see you in my office again. Now get back to your lesson. The next time you see Thompson, I want you to shake hands and make up."

When the bell signaling the end of the school day rang, Alan rushed to the exit. He spotted Paul Thompson and followed him at a distance until they rounded the next corner. Running up to Paul's side he said, "The headmaster suggested we make up."

Paul didn't want to be in Alan's bad books. He clasped the hand offered to him and shook it. Alan waited to make certain Paul was off guard, then, using all his strength, he kneed him in the crotch. He took great delight watching Paul sink slowly to the ground, his face contorted in agony.

* * * *

Most primary school boys in the third and fourth forms had treasured possessions, even though they were of little real value. These included such items as comics, stamps, cigarette cards, marbles, badges, matchbox tops, tin soldiers, and other trinkets. Watching two boys exchange marbles for comics one morning, Alan struck upon an idea. To get started he talked to a number of fellow students, gathering information on their collections and the value they placed on them. Armed with this knowledge, he started brokering trades. This afforded him the opportunity to extract something for himself. Initially, this only produced small rewards, but as his prowess improved, so did the payoffs. By the time he graduated to secondary school at age eleven, he'd earned the nickname, Trader Taylor.

Focusing on trading, Alan abandoned the idea of making money through threats; that is until a new boy named Peter Barrel joined his class. Alan judged Peter to be both weak and feeble. Additionally, he always had money to spend in the tuck shop. Getting Peter alone one break time, a deal was struck, and Peter agreed to make the first payment the following week.

The next morning, Alan took his place in the daily assembly. There, the headmaster addressed the topics of

Spend enough time w/ character
to care about them ?

the day, then led the singing of three hymns and recitation of the Lord's Prayer. At this juncture he normally dismissed the boys. Today he stood with a troubled look on his face.

"I regret having to tell you this. One of our students has behaved in a disgraceful and cowardly manner." He paused. "Consequently, you will all bear witness to his punishment."

Not a murmur could be heard as the headmaster's eyes panned slowly around his audience. Eventually, his gaze honed in on Alan, whom he summoned to the stage with a wag of his finger.

Alan was shocked, wondering what he'd done. *Surely arranging trades wasn't a cowardly matter,* he thought, *and certainly not something that would be considered disgraceful.* Approaching the stage, it slowly registered. He realized he'd misjudged Peter Barrel. With no fanfare or further comment, the headmaster picked up his cane. He gave Alan six strokes—two on each hand, two on his backside. Even the teachers present—most of whom had witnessed canings in the past—had never seen the headmaster deliver punishment with such ferocity. In spite of the pain, Alan remained stone-faced. When he was dismissed, the headmaster saw the same look of defiance he'd seen in the past.

One Monday morning, the geography teacher rushed into the headmaster's study. "Excuse me, sir. One of our pupils has had a nasty accident. I think you need to call an ambulance."

Mr. Gilbert looked up from his desk. "What happened?"

"Class 3B boys were leaving my lesson and heading toward the art room. When they reached the concrete steps, one of them apparently tripped and fell head first down the entire stairway. Mrs. Wilkinson is providing him with first aid. He's badly cut and bruised, and I think his arm is broken."

"What's the boy's name?" the headmaster asked.

"Peter Barrel."

Mr. Gilbert frowned. "Was Alan Taylor in that class by any chance?"

"Funny enough, I thought you might ask that. The answer is no. He's in a two-hour woodwork session."

"All right then, I'll call for an ambulance straight away. See that he gets cared for in the meantime. I'll arrange for someone to deliver a note to his mother."

* * * *

When Peter Barrel returned to school a week later, it was discovered he'd suffered a broken arm, together with severe lacerations to his face and legs requiring numerous stitches. The headmaster met with him on his return, together with several other boys who were present at the scene of the accident. Nobody could offer a clear explanation. One boy said, "It looked like he tripped over someone's foot," and another offered up, "He clipped my arm when he started tumbling forward. I've no idea what caused him to fall in the first place." Even Peter Barrel couldn't provide any useful information. "I know I tripped over something. It happened so quickly, I really don't remember."

Satisfied that it was nothing more than an unfortunate occurrence, Mr. Gilbert wrote a short note to Peter Barrel's parents. He offered condolences for their son's misfortune. He assured them that nobody was to blame.

The day following Mr. Gilbert's enquiry, Alan Taylor met with a classmate, Stan Pickering. Recently, a significant trade had inadvertently revealed that the cricket bat Stan had offered as part of the deal had been stolen from another student. In exchange for silence and a bonus of five shillings, Stan promised to carry out the plan Alan proposed. It would involve enlisting the help of Stan's best friend and would take place at the end of a geography class. When the students approached the concrete steps, Stan would distract Peter, while his friend deftly stuck his foot in front of Peter's ankle. Knowing that the other boys were generally noisy and unfocused travelling between classes, they all agreed that it should be relatively easy to make it look like an accident. Their prediction turned out to be correct.

Alan Taylor learned valuable lessons from his experience with Peter Barrel that would serve him well in the future. Aside from money, he now knew information could also be valuable, and that certain things could be accomplished while letting others do the dirty work.

* * * *

By 1944, Alan had grown to five-feet nine inches, and was one of the tallest boys in his year. On weekends, he watched traders bartering in the local markets and yearned for the opportunity to participate. Bored with academics, he was anxious to get to work. His mother had explained the consequences of breaking the law on many occasions. He knew that leaving school prior to the mandatory age of fourteen could get him into trouble with the police. This was something he wanted to avoid. Concluding that he'd just have to wait it out, an unlikely opportunity arose. Something his mother didn't find out about it until later that summer.

One evening, Daisy was in her living room, talking to a neighbor. Thinking her son to be asleep in bed, she and her visitor talked openly. Though Alan had gone to his room an hour earlier, he was still awake. He hadn't taken much notice of his mother's conversation, thinking it to be senseless gossip. Suddenly, a piece of information grabbed his attention.

For the next few days he kept a look out for Mr. Ken Jones, a man who lived further up the street. One evening, he saw him walking past the house. He ran to his side. When Mr. Jones stopped, Alan asked him to write a letter to his headmaster under the pretext of being his father. The letter should say the family would be moving to Scotland, where Alan would complete his final school year. He also asked Mr. Jones to visit his school and sign any necessary paperwork, sure that this would eliminate any risk to himself.

Mr. Jones listened in total disbelief. "You've got a bloody nerve, you cheeky bugger. Now piss off, or I'll kick your backside." He expected Alan to run away. To his amazement, Alan didn't budge.

clever...
Believable?

"So tell me, Mr. Jones. How would you like your missus to find out you've been fucking Mr. Drummond's wife?"

Mr. Jones went red in the face, offering more threats. Alan stood his ground and adopted a menacing look. Mr. Jones lost his nerve. Two days later, he delivered the letter requested and visited the school to complete the required paperwork.

CHAPTER 5

George Lambert, now twenty-nine years old, could not have been happier with his life. He gained great satisfaction from his work, and he'd long since become Henry's right-hand man. In addition to handling some of the most challenging repairs, he also provided guidance and oversight to young mechanics starting out in the trade. But his greatest joy of all was time spent with family. Every two months, he took Lilly and their daughter, Rita, to visit relatives in the East End, where he reveled in the affection they were always afforded. Most evenings, he spent time reading to his daughter. On Sundays, he and Lilly devoted themselves to keeping her actively occupied visiting places of interest or the local park.

In early 1939, George read the newspaper reports describing the increasingly disturbing events taking place in Europe. He wasn't overly bothered and remained confident that the prime minister would negotiate peace for Great Britain. When the family tuned into their wireless at eleven o'clock on the morning of Sunday, September

3rd, he expected that any outstanding concerns would be put to rest—until Neville Chamberlin uttered the words,

"I have to tell you now that no such undertaking has been received, and that consequently this country is at war with Germany."

Now eight years of age, Rita asked her father what this meant. Sensing her anxiety, George sat her on his lap. "Our soldiers will fight the German soldiers, but there's nothing for you to worry about, my dear. We've done it in the past, and we'll do it again. In any event, your mother and I will always look out for you. There's no need to be concerned." Rita trusted her father implicitly. His assurance was all she needed to feel safe and protected from the world outside.

War brought uncertainty and the nation knuckled down, preparing for the worst. Still in the upper age range for conscripts, George was required to join the reserves. Because his trade was deemed essential, he continued at the repair shop. Beyond conscription age, Henry Wilson was allowed to maintain his business. He was obliged to give priority to emergency transport vehicles.

Following a period of posturing, which later became known as the "phony war," Germany's air force proceeded to inflict terror and destruction on London. One of the prime targets was the dockland area where George and Henry were born. This inspired Henry to join the search and rescue group that went into action at the end of a bombing raid. Their first priority was to save lives. When this phase was complete, they helped with clean up and repair. If he was able to take time off, George joined

Henry on these missions. He witnessed the tragedy of war first-hand—the ruined buildings, the air thick with acrid smoke, and the dangers as people raked through the rubble, risking their lives to help others. Seeing the devastation in the neighborhood where he'd grown up made George sad. He promised himself that if ever the opportunity arose to help with the re-building, he'd jump at it.

In 1945, war finally ended and things started to return to normal. For numerous poor souls, normal had a new definition. The economy had been devastated, causing many firms to experience a dramatic decline in sales. One morning, Henry called George into his office. "I've decided to pursue a different future. I don't think the car repair business will recover for many years."

Henry scratched his chin. "As you know my volunteer work included overseeing the repair of water lines and drains. I met a few tradesmen who were skilled in these areas. I also met several people in positions of influence. With the amount of devastation that's taken place in London and surrounding areas, I think the necessary rebuilding will provide numerous opportunities for plumbing work."

Henry took a deep breath. "You've been loyal to me, so I'd like you to become my right-hand man. I think your talents are applicable, and you have the right personality to manage a work crew. I believe I have a good starting point. Of course there's no guarantee of success. The question is; do you want to join me? Before you answer, you should consider the risk. I won't be offended if you opt for a regular job; I realize you have family to consider. So what do you say? Or do you want more time to think it over?"

George thought for a moment, "Henry, you gave my family the opportunity for a better life. I have every confidence in your plan. Of course I'll join you."

The two had known each other for many years, and their mutual respect had grown strong. Like most men, there was rarely any outward sign of affection. It surprised both of them when in unison they got to their feet and affectionately slapped each other on the back.

* * * *

Wilson Plumbing Company got off to a good start. The division of responsibilities was simple and effective. Henry found new opportunities and negotiated contracts. George scheduled the work and supervised the crews. It was a perfect arrangement. Profits grew steadily, and Henry increased George's compensation accordingly.

At the end of the company's fourth year, Henry recognized George's contribution by making him a junior partner with 10% ownership in the company. On receiving his share of the annual profit, he and Lilly were able to put a deposit on a home of their own—a three-bedroom cottage in a wooded country lane. They counted their blessings, knowing that without family sacrifice and guidance, the lifestyle they were now enjoying would never have been possible.

*   *   *   *

George was now forty-one years old. He found that he was moving a little slower, and that, from all the years lifting produce in the market and working under cars, his shoulders were sometimes stiff with arthritis. His daughter Rita had grown up, become a nurse, and married an auditor at a hospital, Harry Elliott.

In January 1950, George and Lilly celebrated the arrival of their granddaughter, Kate, by holding a small party that Henry and Susan attended. Lilly told George afterward that Susan didn't seem her usual lively self. "Probably just tired from the Christmas and New Year celebrations," George said. Lilly wasn't convinced.

Several days later, Henry asked George to join him in his office. "Shut the door and take a seat, George."

There was nothing unusual about a routine meeting between the two men, but George instinctively felt there was a more serious matter at hand. "I'm afraid I have some bad news. Susan isn't very well. She's been diagnosed with a heart condition. Her doctor says it's an unpredictable ailment. Frankly, I don't think the outlook is promising."

"Oh my god, that's terrible! Is there anything I can possibly do to help?"

"Well, actually there is. I'd like you to take over the business. Given Susan's prognosis, I want to try to do all the things we've dreamed about. I've been able to save a lot of money over the last seven years, so I can afford to take care of her in style. We'd like to spend winters in Spain and summers in the West Country. Of course, we'll be home in between trips, so we'll still see you regularly."

George tried to absorb what he'd just heard. "Henry, you've been generous since the very beginning. We now have our house, and while we've saved a little money, I don't have the means to buy your business."

"My dear George, in asking you to take over the company, I didn't mean that I wanted you to buy it. This is what I'm proposing. You take full control, and we'll agree on your basic salary. Then, whatever profit the business makes, you pay twenty-five percent of it to me. I'm confident that will give me a good income for the future. So what do you say?"

"How could I possibly accept your offer? It's not fair to you. You own ninety percent of the firm, so you could get a much better deal elsewhere."

"If I sold my shares to someone else, there's no telling what might happen. You deserve much better than that. The success of Wilson Plumbing is in large part due to your efforts. Additionally, as Susan and I have never been blessed with children, it keeps the company in the family. What I'm proposing allows things to continue without interference from the outside, and, in effect, gives me the equivalent of an early pension. Don't underestimate yourself, George. What I'm proposing should actually work well for both of us."

Henry's words ran through George's mind. He felt eternally indebted and didn't wish to take advantage of the situation. On the other hand, he realized a source of income would help Henry fulfill his plans for Susan. He also understood the pride Henry took in the company and would want it to continue in the same manner.

Overwhelmed, George took a shaky breath. "Henry, I will gratefully accept your proposal, subject to one adjustment."

Henry looked surprised, "What might that be?" he asked.

"That the profit be split fifty-fifty."

Henry broke into a broad smile and then started laughing. "You're negotiating on my behalf instead of your own. At the same time, it only confirms what I've always admired about you. I'll tell you what, why don't we meet halfway?

George quickly got into the spirit of the moment. Following a round of playful haggling, they respectfully agreed on a forty-sixty split.

Ten days later, Henry collected the documents his solicitor had prepared that set out terms of the new arrangement. He proposed changing the company name to Wilson and Lambert Plumbing. George wouldn't hear of it. In his heart and mind it would always be the Wilson Plumbing Company, and Henry reluctantly gave in to his wishes. The following weekend both men and their wives met to celebrate Henry and Susan's upcoming trip to Spain. They enjoyed a congenial evening together; though Lilly didn't think Susan looked well and prayed her health would improve.

It didn't take long for George to realize just how much Henry had meant to the firm, in particular the new business he'd always secured. Working methodically and with Lilly's support, the situation gradually righted itself. Apart from the satisfaction George gained from the successful continuation of the firm, his highlight occurred at the end of each month. This was when the profit was calculated and forty percent of it forwarded to his friend and partner, Henry.

* * * *

Approaching her fourth birthday, Kate decided there were only four important people in the world—Mummy, Daddy, Grandma, and Grandpa, especially Grandpa. Grandma made the most wonderful cakes for tea, but Grandpa—Grandpa was the special one. Most weekends Kate visited her grandparents, often the highlight of her week. On arrival, Grandpa would give her a big hug, sit her down beside him, and read to her or tell stories. Sometimes, these would be funny ones about her mother, which would make them both laugh hysterically. With story time over, they'd play games—Kate's favorites were hide-and-seek and horsey. Kate was always the one to hide, and would normally go straight to the kitchen where her Grandma would find a good spot. When her Grandpa entered the room, he would noisily bang around, constantly asking "Where's Kate? Have you seen Kate?" eventually calling out "Kate, are you in here?" Despite her Grandma putting a finger to her lips, Kate would cry out, "No Grandpa, I'm not in here; you have to look elsewhere."

"All right then, I'll try another room," would be the reply, a response that caused Kate to giggle uncontrollably. After playtime, George took his granddaughter for ice cream or a fruit lollipop. An afternoon with Grandpa was filled with fun, and Kate always hoped the day could last longer.

Now that Lilly only worked mornings, she was able to arrange for Kate's fourth birthday party to be held at their home. George took the afternoon off, and since the weather stayed fine, he organized games for Kate and her friends outside in the garden. It gave Rita great pleasure to see her daughter playing happily, and served as a reminder of her caring parents. Harry was able to join the party and afterward he took the whole family for an early dinner.

Recently, Harry had been promoted, and his responsibilities now extended to other medical facilities. This required him to travel and sometimes be away overnight. Rita was uncomfortable with her husband's absence, and on such occasions she and Kate stayed at her parents' home. Harry was sensitive to his wife's discomfort, so unless it was completely unavoidable, he drove home even if it meant arriving late in the evening.

One Wednesday, Harry was required to visit a hospital in Sussex. Rita knew he would be late home, so she fed Kate and had her in bed by seven-thirty. To pass the time she curled up in an armchair and began reading a book. At eight-thirty, she heard the doorbell ring. Thinking Harry had forgotten his key, she ran to open the door, only to find a police officer standing there.

"Good evening, Madam. I'm Constable Burrows. Are you Mrs. Rita Elliott?"

"Yes," Rita replied.

"Mrs. Elliott, there's something I need to talk to you about. Do you mind if I come inside?"

She led him into the sitting room, her mind racing and fear gripping her body.

"Mrs. Elliott, I'm afraid I have bad news. About one hour ago, your husband was in a car crash on the A127 road."

Rita stared at him in terror. The unthinkable came to mind, though she tried hard to push it away. The effort made her queasy. "Was he…" she could hardly get the words out, "Was he seriously injured?" She prayed the constable would say, "Don't worry, your husband is alive and will fully recover." Constable Burroughs swallowed. "I'm terribly sorry Mrs. Elliott. Your husband was killed outright."

Rita went into shock. She couldn't comprehend the constable's words. Surely there was some mistake. Her face turned deathly white. Her lips moved, though words were not forthcoming. PC Burrows recognized her condition and called for an ambulance. Fortunately, he was able to elicit her parent's telephone number.

On hearing the news, George and Lilly rushed over to Rita's house and spent the night deliberating on what they'd tell Kate the following morning. Lilly decided it would be best to say her mother wasn't feeling well, and they would be going back to their house for a while. She asked George to talk with Kate when they got an update on Rita's condition.

At six o'clock the next morning, George arrived at the hospital. The doctor had completed his evaluation, and decided to keep Rita for another forty-eight hours in order to monitor her progress. Lilly took Kate home, and when George returned, she asked him to explain to their granddaughter what had happened to her father. He didn't relish the task. He knew it was his duty, and he'd carry it out to the best of his ability. He took Kate into the bedroom and sat her on the end of the bed. There, he took a deep breath, trying to hide his sadness. "Kate, I have something to tell you."

"What is it, Grandpa?"

"Yesterday, your daddy was in an accident. He loves you Kate and always will. Now he's in heaven."

"When will he come back, Grandpa?"

"Well, he'll be gone for a long time because he's now with God. He'll always be looking out for you."

"That's not fair! I want to see my daddy now," Kate said, throwing her arms around George's neck and sobbing violently. George didn't think further explanation would help. He took Kate in his arms and lay beside her until she cried herself to sleep.

On Saturday morning, George collected Rita from the hospital. She was responsive to questions and attentive to Kate, though quiet and distant. George and Lilly thought this understandable and knew it would take time for her to heal. Regrettably, even several months later, there was little improvement. George cancelled Rita's rental agreement, and she and Kate moved in with them.

* * * *

Wilson Plumbing's reputation and work volume continued to grow. In the process, George saw changes occurring in the industry that required new and improved skills. He realized education was becoming more and more important if children were to succeed in the workplace. He wanted to do everything possible to give Kate the best start in life. Certain she was intelligent enough to attend university, he and Lilly set up a savings plan to pay for school fees and expenses. They were confident that given the appropriate support and opportunity, a bright future lay ahead of their granddaughter.

CHAPTER

Daisy sat in her rumpled dressing gown. She hadn't been able to sleep well despite having taken two pills that were supposed to help. Her mouth felt thick and furry, and her head ached. She looked at the clock. Nearly eight o'clock. She frowned. The summer holidays were over and school started again today. Alan had only one hour to get there, or he would be punished for being tardy. She went to his door for the third time and banged on it hard. "Wake up, or you'll be late," she called out.

Moments later, her son appeared wearing his pajamas. "What's all the fuss about?"

"Have you forgotten what day it is? School starts back today."

Alan shrugged. "I left two months ago. I'm a working man now."

"What do you mean? You're only 13! How many times do I have to tell you? You need to stay at school until you're fourteen, or you'll be breaking the law."

"Well, that's my business," he said, sitting down and buttering a slice of toast.

"I don't know what you're playing at young man. It's also my business. If you miss school, the truant officer will be paying us a visit. Do you want us both to get into trouble?"

"You worry too much. In any event, I've taken care of things. You won't be hearing from the school because they think we've moved to Scotland," Alan replied, putting his feet up on the settee and biting into his breakfast.

"I've a feeling you've been up to no good. Why would your school think we've moved? I've warned you about your behavior. This sort of attitude will come back to haunt you."

Alan smirked. "You're a fine one to talk."

Daisy stood up and glared at her son. "What the hell's that supposed to mean?"

"Look, you've always told me you were a hostess and dancer. I guess you thought I'd never find out. I've known for years that you're a stripper, and that you let men fuck you for money. And now you're talking about *my* behavior."

Daisy was stunned. She had always known the truth may eventually come to light. She hadn't prepared herself for the possibility. She hesitated, trying to think of an explanation. "Look, I never wanted to do this job. I only did it for you. It was the only way I could put a roof over your head." She paused. "And avoid sending you off to an orphanage."

Alan scoffed. "You still assume I know nothing about my background. Well, I do. You could have tried keeping your legs crossed in the first place. Then you wouldn't have had me to worry about."

"Don't talk to me like that you little bugger!" she screamed, tears stinging her eyes.

Alan gave his mother a disdainful look and headed back to his bedroom.

"Where are you going?" Daisy shouted.

"To get dressed and then off to make some money," he yelled back at her.

Minutes later Daisy heard the front door slam shut. She let out a loud sigh, flopped into the armchair and stared at the ceiling, reflecting on the years since Alan had become part of her life. *Oh hell*, she thought. *What a terrible mother I've been, a total failure.* It had been so hard and Alan had always been such a difficult boy. She knew she should have spent more time with him, and the absence of a father only added to the difficulty of enforcing discipline.

Her thoughts briefly turned to Derek. She'd tried hard to put him completely out of her mind, but there was always the odd occasion when his memory surfaced. Despite the passage of time, her feelings of resentment toward him had never lessened. She also knew that dealing with the indignities of her profession had played a large role, particularly the habits it had led to in order for her to cope. *What a bloody mess my life is,* she thought. What could she do? Just carrying on was her only option, and if nothing else, she still had her son. Hopefully the rift that had developed between them would heal eventually.

* * * *

Seeking to make a living, Alan found a niche trading broken or damaged goods that could be mended and sold on. Over the following couple of years this provided enough money to survive, but he soon realized it wouldn't take him where he wanted to go. Gaining insight into the lifestyles of wealthy traders only acted to strengthen his ambitions.

With war over, both politicians and industrialists alike predicted better times ahead. While encouraged, Alan knew he needed to accumulate cash for investment if he was going to progress. Regular employment, with fixed compensation, didn't seem to be the answer; in any event he had no tangible marketable skills. A discussion with a boy he'd befriended at the market caused him to reconsider.

"I know you're always looking for earners. My elder brother made enough money working in a petrol station to start his own business."

"A job like that pays low wages. How could you possibly save money?" Alan replied, thinking his acquaintance must be mistaken.

"It wasn't all on the straight and narrow, but nothing that would get you into serious trouble. I know that's something you want to avoid."

"How did he do it, then?"

"I don't know the details. I could introduce you to my brother if you want. I'm sure he'd be happy to give you the low down."

At a meeting with his friend's brother, Alan learned about the schemes he'd been engaged in. He was intrigued. While the ideas appeared to be practical, there was a drawback. It would require cooperation in order to be implemented, and it may be tough to find a willing accomplice.

Most petrol stations employed a forecourt attendant and typically a youngster to help him. At certain times of the day, business was heavier than one person could effectively handle. If customers found a queue, they would invariably go elsewhere, often never to return. Because wages for a junior helper were low, openings frequently cropped up.

Alan responded to a number of vacancies. He hadn't been able to find a forecourt attendant who might be a good fit; that is, until he met Harvey Murray. Harvey was a short, stocky individual with a pronounced beer belly. Somehow, he'd managed to bumble along happily through life without ever exerting himself, and he intended to continue doing so. His wife didn't ask for much and this suited Harvey, who liked to spend evenings in the pub, studying form for his weekly visit to the bookmakers.

"Is the helper position still open?" Alan asked the man sitting on a chair outside the station office smoking a cigarette.

"Yes, son, it is," Harvey replied. He stood up, which appeared to take some effort on his part. Alan was now more than six feet tall and towered over the man in front of him.

"Why don't you come into the office and we can talk? You'll have to excuse me if customers arrive." Alan followed Harvey into the office where he explained the work hours and pay. "And normally you'll get a few tips," he added, hoping this would be an inducement if the young man he was interviewing seemed suitable. Alan's gut told him he may have found a suitable "partner". He used all his charm, enquiring about Harvey's interests and paying compliments wherever possible. Harvey was flattered and offered Alan the job.

"Well, that sounds great. When would you like me to start?"

"Let's make it seven thirty tomorrow morning!"

* * * *

Alan arrived early and worked diligently in order to make life easy for Harvey. Within a few days his initial assessment was confirmed; Harvey was gullible, lazy, and perhaps, more importantly, he had few scruples.

There wasn't much to learn about the job, though Alan paid particular attention to the delivery tankers and those customers who requested their oil be checked. At the conclusion of his first week, he was confident his plan could be successfully implemented. The remaining challenge was—would Harvey go along with it?

At six o'clock on Saturday afternoon, Harvey put the CLOSED sign in the forecourt entryway. "Enjoy your day off, and I'll see you Monday," he called out.

"I look forward to it. By the way, do you have time for a quick pint?" Alan asked, holding up his first pay packet.

Harvey happily accepted, having never refused a drink in his life. Alan purchased two pints of bitter and found a table where they could talk in private. Seeing no point in dragging things out, he outlined his plan. "Remember Harvey, your role won't change at all. I'll take care of everything. I've done some calculations, and I estimate that at the end of the day, your wages will effectively double."

The proposition had Harvey's full attention. He pondered over it while casually tapping his glass, hoping Alan would notice it was empty. "Is there any chance we might get into trouble?" he asked, when Alan returned from the bar with two more drinks.

"No, Harvey. Think about it, who's getting hurt? The answer is nobody. In fact, the owner gets higher sales and customers benefit from better service. Its win-win all 'round."

"What if they find out we're shorting them?"

"It's only a tiny bit, they'll never notice. And look, if anyone ever complains, I'll take the rap, I promise. After all, you could always say you didn't know what I was up to."

Harvey reflected. He could see the potential and tried to weigh the risk. Likely, he thought, the upside had been exaggerated. Overall, he couldn't see a downside, especially with Alan carrying the can if things went awry. "All right, son," he said, swallowing the remainder of his second pint and indicating that his glass was empty again.

* * * *

At seven o'clock on Monday morning, Alan let himself into the station office and unlatched the supply room door. In the far corner he placed the metal tray he'd collected from the market the previous day, and then covered it with heavy gauge mesh. Using a screwdriver, he removed the front cover of a forecourt petrol pump and practiced turning the consumption dials back and forth. When Harvey strolled in at seven-thirty, Alan had everything prepared, including a mug of tea for his new 'partner.' The two of them made small talk until the first customer pulled in, at which time Alan reminded Harvey of the routine.

"Good morning sir, how can we help you today?" Harvey asked the clean cut gentleman who'd rolled down the window of his Ford Prefect.

"I'd like four gallons of 101 octane grade, please."

Harvey engaged the customer in conversation, while Alan pumped the petrol. With the order fulfilled, Harvey asked, "Can we check your oil today, sir?"

"Yes, thank you," he replied.

Harvey nodded at Alan, who opened the car bonnet, removed the dipstick and wiped it clean. Then, out of sight from the customer, he placed two fingers at the top of the rod and reinserted it into its tube. He knew from his meeting with his friend's brother that this shortened the reading by a little more than half a pint.

"Not dangerously low, but I'd recommend a pint, sir." Harvey said with some authority upon seeing the result of Alan's work.

"Of course," the gentleman responded. "No point in taking chances."

At Harvey's direction Alan collected a can from the oil rack, removed the tab and began pouring it into the engine. When the flow slowed to a dribble he turned the can through 180 degrees, causing the remaining drops to be trapped behind the lid.

Pleased with the attention he'd received, the gentleman gave Harvey a sixpenny tip. "The service has got a lot better since the last time I came here. I'll tell my friends about it," he said, winding up his window and waving as he drove away.

During a lull in business, Alan took the empty oil cans they'd accumulated into the supply room. Using a nail punch and hammer, he made several holes in each lid. Then he placed the cans upside down on the mesh covering the metal tray. By days end their oil sales were double the normal. So were their tips. In addition, Alan was able to fill a gallon can with fresh oil residue.

On Wednesday morning, the delivery tanker arrived. Alan greeted the driver and invited him into the back room for a cup of tea and a chat. Ten minutes later, a deal was struck. It had been established that the tanker carried twenty-five gallons more than the purchase consignment—a contingency against evaporation or minor spillage in the unloading process. In exchange for a bottle of scotch, the driver agreed to pump an additional fifteen gallons into the underground storage tank on each of his twice a week visits.

At the end of the day's business, Alan removed the front cover from one of the petrol pumps and turned the consumption dial back by fifteen gallons. He'd learned that this would allow him to pocket the money from the corresponding sales the following day, without detection.

With the work week over, Alan took Harvey for a drink. He provided details of the earnings from the petrol scam and the second-hand oil he sold to an acquaintance in the market. Harvey could barely believe his ears. His regular wage was almost doubled, let alone the additional tip money they divided on a daily basis.

For the first time in his life, Alan had cash to spare. He purchased fashionable clothes—something he enjoyed displaying—and frequented pubs and cafes. With an eye toward his future ambitions, he also opened a savings account at the post office. One evening on a night out, he bumped into an old acquaintance. In the course of their conversation, he was asked, "Alan, my flat mate is getting married shortly and then he'll be moving out. I'm looking for someone to take his place. Do you have any interest? If you do, you'll have your own bedroom, which has definite advantages." He nodded in the direction of two young women who'd been making eyes at them.

Moving out from his mother's home was something Alan had never considered. Though his feelings toward her were indifferent at best, living together was all he'd ever known. "I'll think about it," he said. He hadn't taken the offer seriously at the time, but waking up the following morning alongside one of the girls he'd met the previous evening made his decision easy.

Daisy was upset by her son's plan. She'd known such a day would surely have to come. She assumed it wouldn't happen before he married. "Why do you want to move out?" she asked, dreading the thought of being separated. "You've got everything you need here, and you've had your own room since grandma passed away. If I'm interfering with your social life, I don't mind if you have friends around."

"It's not that; I just need my own space, Mum."

Guessing at her son's true motivation, Daisy added, "Look, if you want to bring a girl home and have time alone, I could always go out for the evening."

"It's not the same thing and you know it. In any event, I'm only moving a few blocks away. It's not like I'm going off to another country."

Daisy sat down trying to calm herself. Soon the tears started flowing. In a rare display of affection, Alan sat beside his mother and put an arm around her shoulder. "Look, I'll still visit. And come to that, you'll be able to pop over to my place whenever you like."

Daisy was lost for words. She smiled through her tears and hugged Alan tightly, not wanting to let him go. "I can't stop you. If you must go, take care of yourself, my darling. I wish things could have been different. I've always loved you with all of my heart, and I only ever wanted the best for you."

* * * *

Since Alan's departure, Daisy found herself with more time on her hands. No longer needing to get home at any particular hour, she started going out with Penny Trent, a co-performer. She'd known Penny throughout her time at the club and the two of them were the longest serving members. They'd always got along well. Now that they were meeting outside the club, their friendship grew

Efficient story-telling

closer. One Saturday, following a fish and chip supper, they went back to Daisy's flat for coffee. They talked past midnight, and now having a spare room, Daisy suggested Penny spend the night. Penny agreed, and the two women ended up having so much fun that Daisy invited her to stay for the remainder of the weekend. The weekend stretched into the following week, and by the end of the month, Penny had become a permanent fixture.

It was, Daisy decided, the best decision she could have possibly made. She enjoyed having company. Her marriage and subsequent experience working in the Sunlight Club had convinced her that she no longer wanted or needed another man in her life. Their relationship prospered. Soon, Daisy couldn't even remember when feisty Penny, with her quirky sense of humor and endless cups of tea, hadn't been part of her life.

* * * *

Christened Penelope Victoria Trent, daughter of an unwed farm worker, Penny was sent to an orphanage at three months of age. There she stayed for thirteen years, at which time the institution sent her to work at the local manor house. Initially the housekeeper was welcoming and helped Penny settle in. One night, several months later, everything changed. Cozied up in bed, Penny heard a light tap on her door, and moments later the housekeeper appeared,

"I've come to wish you goodnight my dear," she said, sitting next to Penny and kissing her lightly on the cheek.

Being devoid of physical affection in her early life, Penny was touched. She assumed the housekeeper had just popped in and would leave shortly. Instead, she smiled sweetly, sat on the side of the bed, and gently slid one hand under the sheets, placing it between Penny's thighs. Shocked and frightened, Penny hastily pushed the housekeeper away with both hands, causing her to fall backwards onto the floor. When she got up, her serene smile turned to a look of thunder. "You ungrateful bitch, you'll live to regret this night," she spat out through clenched teeth.

From that moment on, Penny was given the worst of chores and subjected to relentless criticism. Being a junior, there was no avenue to seek recourse and her life became a living hell. She tolerated her predicament, not seeing any practical alternative. Several months later, she befriended the stable boy. A conversation with him gave her reason to be more optimistic about the future. He did follow up on the promises he'd made. Unfortunately, they didn't bring about the results she'd hoped for. "I'm sorry, Penny. I've run into a problem. The few openings that I thought might work for you have a requirement that I hadn't anticipated."

"What do you mean?" Penny asked. She tried to prepare herself for the disappointment she felt coming.

"They all require a suitable referral from the housekeeper. Based on what you've told me, it's obvious that she wouldn't give you one."

Penny was distraught. "I suppose I'm struck in this hell-hole for the rest of my days," she said with tears trickling down her cheeks."

The stable boy had become very fond of Penny. He was upset by his inability to help her. "I know this isn't what you'd hoped for. Honestly, I tried my best. It's just that they all said the same thing." He hesitated and blushed.

"What is it?" Penny asked, "I've a feeling you're holding something back."

"Well, there was one opening that the blacksmith told me about. It's just not something suitable for you."

Penny's interest was aroused. "Shouldn't I be the judge of that?"

"It's too embarrassing to mention."

The stable boy stared at the floor in silence.

"Are you going to tell me or not?" Penny asked.

"There's a strip club in the docklands that hires pretty young girls like you." He exclaimed, his face turning bright red.

In different circumstances, Penny would have been insulted. She knew the stable boy only had good intentions and that she herself had pushed him to reveal a subject he'd been embarrassed by. She laughed it off, saying, "You're just a dirty little sod."

Hoping things would improve over time, Penny tried to "grin and bear" her grim existence. In fact, matters went from bad to worse. Desperation came into play, and following an overnight disappearing act, she made her debut at the Sunlight Club.

CHAPTER

Alan Taylor celebrated his first anniversary at the petrol station with a man who'd benefitted from his second-hand oil business. Over a beer, his new pal told him. "It's been great doing business with you. I don't know if you're looking for other ventures. I've heard, 'there's money in muck.' If you're interested, I could probably help."

"How do you mean?" Alan asked; he'd never heard the expression.

"Well, there's construction going on all across London. And because of the war damage, I think it will continue for years to come. All the sites want debris or excavated earth hauled away. If you've got a lorry, it's easy to get work. From what I understand there's also some angles to make a few extras."

Alan's ears pricked up, "I like the sound of that," he said, keen to hear more. His pal told him what he knew about the haulage business and offered to make an introduction to a relative, an employee at the local council. The following week, Alan met his friend's cousin who provided information on how to secure contracts. He also hinted at ways to enhance one's rewards. Alan took careful note. When he'd weighed up the pros and cons he decided this line of business offered more potential than his current job. Using his savings, he was able to make a down payment on a second-hand lorry. Armed with the necessary equipment, he attended an interview with his friend's cousin, which resulted in him being awarded a contract in South London. The project involved excavation for an underground parking garage that would take four or five months to complete. Compensation was on a piece-work system, which meant getting paid for the number of loads hauled from the site to the tip.

Following the award, his friend's cousin took him to one side, saying. "If I were you, I'd meet with the site timekeeper. I think you'll find it beneficial. He'll be at the Coach and Horses pub tonight. I can introduce you."

Alan spent a pleasant evening over drinks and learned more about the council's business procedures. With terms agreed, he shook the timekeeper's hand and wished him a pleasant night.

The established procedure required every driver to secure a signed docket, recording the time and vehicle license plate number for every load taken from the site. In Alan's case, the timekeeper advanced the actual time by ten minutes on the first docket, twenty minutes on the second, and so on. At day's end, Alan had artificially made up two hours. This allowed the timekeeper to give him two additional dockets, showing a one-hour difference between each of them.

Signed dockets were used to support invoices, which gave Alan the ability to bill for twelve additional loads every week. On top of this, he also got reimbursed for dump charges. He was able to invoice for twelve more of these as well. Upon receiving his weekly check, he gave the timekeeper the agreed share. Alan had done quite well at the petrol station. Now he'd moved up a notch, and as a bonus, the scheme was effectively risk free.

Checking invoices was the responsibility of the council accountant. He had no authority over the timekeeper. He could only raise a red flag if something seemed out of order. In Alan's case, there was nothing that appeared improper, just that his turnaround was faster than most. Additionally, if the scam was ever uncovered, it would have to involve the timekeeper because he'd signed the dockets. On a practical matter, the Council Public Works manager would never allow one of his staff to be prosecuted—it would reflect badly on the department.

* * * *

Penny settled into her new life sharing a home with Daisy. Over time, their conversations touched on more personal matters. Daisy told her all about her son and what a good boy he really was. She blamed herself for any shortcomings he may have. Penny saw things differently. She thought that behind the charm there was a different person; one that she didn't much care for or trust. She kept her thoughts to herself; she knew raising them would only cause a rift with Daisy, something she was keen to avoid.

In 1949, Daisy had her thirty-fifth birthday. Penny took her out for dinner to celebrate. They were enjoying a pleasant evening when suddenly Daisy jumped up and rushed to the bathroom. Penny followed behind to find Daisy throwing up in the sink—something that had happened several times recently. "You really should see a doctor. I'm getting worried about you," Penny said, touching Daisy's arm lightly.

"Oh, it's nothing. Probably the fish was off," Daisy replied, dismissing the subject out of hand.

Penny decided not to pursue the matter. She'd come to understand how cantankerous Daisy could be when it came to her health. But it didn't stop Penny from worrying about her dear friend.

* * * *

Alan's haulage business continued to be successful. Completing his third contract, he'd accumulated enough cash to acquire another lorry and hire a driver. The resulting income enabled him to upgrade his lifestyle and expand his network while still adding to his savings. Though he was pleased with his progress, it only acted to further fuel his ambitions. Driving onto a new project one morning, he had a chance conversation with a building contractor. The outcome of their meeting resulted in him picturing bigger possibilities for his future. He was confident he could secure work in a new line of business. The challenge would be getting the specialist assistance required to make it successful.

One evening in May, Alan found himself at a loose end. A date with a girl had fallen through, and he wasn't sure what to do with the rest of the evening. He decided it was a good time to visit his mother, especially needing to get some washing seen to. Daisy opened the door to find Alan handing over his laundry bag. "Hello, Mum," he said cheerfully. "I thought I'd take you and Penny down the local for a couple of drinks."

Daisy took the bag and gave him a hug. "I'm so sorry, love. I'm not feeling my best—it's that silly upset stomach again. Why don't you take Penny? I'm sure she'd like a night out."

Penny shook her head. "Oh, no; I couldn't go without you."

Alan didn't relish the prospect of spending the evening on his own. "Oh, come on, Penny," he said with his most winsome smile. "It's our chance to get to know each other a little bit better."

"Yes, do go, Penny," Daisy insisted. "I'm just going to be lying down. I won't be good company tonight."

Penny reluctantly agreed, and she and Alan set off to the Green Man Pub. Penny had become cautious of Alan since living with Daisy. For Daisy's sake, and because she'd agreed to go out with him, she was determined to make the evening pleasant.

Alan returned from the bar carrying their second round of drinks. "So," Penny said brightly, "how's your business going?"

Alan shrugged, "No complaints, but it's levelled off lately. I've been thinking about another line with bigger opportunities."

"Really, what do you have in mind?"

"I'm looking at the building industry. It seems like it's on the up and up."

Penny was surprised. "Why, I didn't know you had the training."

Alan laughed. "I don't. I want to be a contractor. I'll get the jobs and hire somebody else to manage the work."

The statement stirred Penny's memory. "Do you have anyone in mind?" she asked.

Alan looked up sharply, arrested by something in her tone. "No, I don't. Why? Do you know of anybody?"

Penny nodded slowly. "Funny enough, I just might."

CHAPTER 8

Born in Guilford, Surrey, in 1907, Francis (Frank) Ward was the only child of Trevor Ward and his wife, Victoria (formerly Chatfield). Trevor was a teacher at a local grammar school. Victoria lived the life of a socialite.

The Ward's had never pretended to be in love. Their marriage was a convenient way to fulfill individual needs. Victoria's father, Richard Chatfield, knew his daughter's true feelings. When he discovered his son was infertile, he wanted Victoria to provide him with a grandson. Richard knew that his daughter yearned to maintain the lifestyle that his considerable wealth had provided. He used this knowledge to accomplish his own desires.

Trevor Ward came from a respectable family that had lost their wealth through bad investments. Given the prevailing circumstances, it didn't take Richard long to make arrangements that satisfied his own goals along with those of his daughter and Trevor.

* * * *

Following his birth, Frank Ward was immediately put into the full-time care of a live-in nanny, a certain Miss Hodges. His mother believed her only responsibilities were to provide him with hired supervision and give criteria for acceptable behavior and pursuits. In other circumstances his father would have liked to have been more involved in his son's life. He'd already learned not to cross his wife and to steer away from anything that would jeopardize the terms he'd agreed to with his father-in-law.

Being a school teacher, Trevor Ward had hoped that his son would follow in his footsteps. His wife had made in clear from the beginning that Frank's destiny was to work in the family business under the direction of her brother. Still keen to win his mother's love and attention, despite constant neglect, Frank found himself reluctantly agreeing to her wishes.

In 1923, Frank joined the family business. The firm had developed a sterling reputation during its sixty-year history, and its success had underpinned the Chatfield family fortune. Victoria's brother, Len Chatfield, was now running day-to-day operations, allowing their father to slowly work his way into retirement. Frank quickly discovered that like his mother, Len was reserved, bad tempered, arrogant, and demanding.

Reaching his early twenties, Frank pursued the company of several young ladies. To his dismay, none of them met with his mother's approval. Instead, Victoria Ward introduced her son to the local librarian, a young lady she thought suitable to join the family. Finally giving in to unrelenting pressure, Frank married Emma Parsons in March, 1930.

Later in the year, the newspapers started writing articles about the downturn in the economy. The Chatfield's assumed this to be a short term dip that would pass quickly. Like most others, they underestimated its enormity. By 1932, they had no alternative other than to take drastic measures to keep the company afloat.

The arrival of 1933 brought even more distress when two major contracts were cancelled through lack of funds. The unthinkable stared Richard Chatfield in the face. In a desperate, last-ditch effort to avoid bankruptcy, he contacted old friends from his army days, seeking their assistance. Fortunately, this led to a new contract in South London. Despite the firm's dire position, Len Chatfield was not prepared to surrender his pampered lifestyle. Instead, he directed his nephew, Frank, to relocate in order to manage the project.

To his chagrin, Frank discovered that his wife was also unwilling to move, causing him to rent a small apartment in Battersea on his own. He'd known for some while that his marriage was not working the way he'd wished. He clung onto the hope that spending weekdays apart may bring him and his wife closer together. Regrettably, this was not to be the case. It soon became clear that Emma, like his mother, was primarily interested in socializing and didn't much care whether he visited on weekends or not.

Weeks turned into months, and given his wife's attitude, Frank started going home less often. With time on his hands, he focused on securing new business. Prior to living in London, Frank rarely touched alcohol. Now, he was entertaining potential clients, he found himself developing a taste for fine wines and single malt whiskey.

In pursuit of a large project, Frank invited the owner's representative to join him for lunch at a popular seafood restaurant. The gentleman accepted the invitation, but proposed an alternate location in the East End. When Frank's taxi pulled up outside the Sunlight Club, he wondered what the possible attraction could be. It was a converted storage building located in a rundown industrial area close to the docks. Thirty minutes later, his question was answered.

Over lunch, Frank and his guest consumed several glasses of wine followed by two double whiskeys. On their journey back, they talked about the performers and, emboldened by alcohol, their conversation was sprinkled with lewd remarks and innuendos.

Returning to his office the following morning, Frank was suffering from a hangover. He hoped its root cause had improved his chances of winning the project. Consequently, he was optimistic when his receptionist told him Dan Harris was on the line. "Frank, I had a great time yesterday. We think alike and I'm sure we'll work well together. I'd like to arrange a meeting with a couple of my colleagues to discuss next steps."

Frank could hardly contain himself. "That's wonderful news, Dan. Thank you for having confidence in our firm. I also enjoyed myself. Great recommendation, if I might say so. Perhaps we could do it again sometime?"

"I'd like that. By the way, I've been a frequent visitor to the Sunlight Club for several years, so I know the manager quite well. I called him this morning and I've arranged a little surprise for you. You could call it a treat."

"Really, what might that be?" Frank asked; his curiosity aroused.

"Drop by the club tomorrow for lunch and watch the show. At two-thirty, go upstairs to the manager's office and introduce yourself. He'll show you into a private room where you can meet Penny."

"Who's Penny?"

"She's the young lady you were drooling over yesterday. You know, the one with long legs and blonde hair, although that of course was a wig."

"Surely you're kidding me."

"I'm certainly not. And by the way, this is strictly between us boys, something I will never mention to anyone. You have my word on that. I've taken care of the arrangements. All you have to do is show up and enjoy yourself."

Frank was flummoxed, and he still hadn't spoken another word when Dan wished him a good day and hung up.

*　*　*　*

The following morning, Frank felt lethargic. He hadn't been able to sleep properly; he couldn't get his mind away from the arrangement that Dan Harris had made. By mid-morning, Frank had decided visiting Penny was inappropriate, and that he would make up some excuse.

But lust got the better of him, and at eleven-thirty, he found himself hailing a taxi. Upon arrival at the Sunlight Club, Frank ordered a large whiskey and took a seat, just three rows back from the stage.

Like his previous visit, he was hypnotized by the young women stripping. His excitement reached a new level when Penny appeared. At the conclusion of her performance, Frank wondered if he had the nerve to go ahead with the plan. To strengthen his resolve, he consumed another large whiskey.

Setting eyes on Penny, made Frank wish he'd drank less. The blond wig she wore on stage had been removed to reveal her natural light-brown hair, which Frank thought made her look even more attractive. "Can I pour you a drink?" she asked, pointing at the bottles sitting on the side table. Frank knew he'd already had enough, but still found himself saying, "I'll have a whiskey, please."

Penny poured two drinks and toasted her guest. Then she sat on the edge of the bed. "Do you live around these parts? I haven't seen you here before."

"I live in Battersea. It's only a short-term arrangement. My permanent home is in Surrey," Frank replied, desperately trying not to slur his words.

"Well," Penny said, handing Frank a condom, "we only have thirty minutes. I suggest we get started."

Despite his desire, Frank knew the alcohol he'd consumed would prevent his body from cooperating. Penny had experienced this situation on many occasions. Recognizing Frank's condition, she said, "Is there anything I can do to please you?"

"I just wanted to see how beautiful you are up close. And I must say that I'm not disappointed. I'll take my leave now," Frank said, kissing Penny's cheek on his way out. Penny was dumbfounded.

I thought I'd experienced everything possible in this profession, she mused. *Then someone goes and surprises you again!*

* * * *

In the days following Frank's visit to the Sunlight Club, he couldn't get the image of Penny out from his mind. The physical attraction was easy to understand, but there was something else about her that he was pulled toward. He reminded himself that she was a stripper and prostitute who wouldn't give him the time of day if she weren't being paid. That didn't dampen his fascination, and against his better judgement, he made another appointment. This time, he promised himself to remain sober, and although he consumed a large whiskey to calm his nerves, he kept his senses intact. Like the previous visit, Penny offered him a drink, which he refused, suggesting they get down to business.

* * * *

On his way back to the office, Frank reflected on what had just taken place. Clearly his lust had been satisfied, but he felt empty. Yes, he had wanted to make love to Penny. The knowledge that she was simply doing her job frustrated him. He wanted to know more about her and understand the underlying reason for his attraction. On subsequent visits, he tried hard to build a relationship. He often chose to spend his allotted time just talking. For her part, Penny found this rather strange; not sure what to make of it.

* * * *

In 1939, Great Britain declared war on Germany in response to their invasion of Poland. Because of past relationships, Richard Chatfield was directed to have his London-based business assigned to the Royal Engineers based in Chatham, Kent. He put his grandson in charge of operations. For the next six years Frank was preoccupied with urgent wartime needs; primarily repairing military facilities that had been damaged and building temporary housing and shelters. Fully aware of his responsibilities, Frank refrained from his pre-war habits and led both a sober and celibate existence.

Finally, in 1945, war came to an end, and Frank turned his attention back to the family business. He'd been able to maintain a few of his contacts, so it didn't take long to get things moving again. While Frank was still married, it now amounted to little more than a legal contract. His visits home were increasingly infrequent and were invariably lonely and frustrating experiences. Divorce crossed his mind. He dreaded the prospect and expected it would be made painful by all involved.

At a loss to find happiness, Frank threw himself into his work. He also resumed his heavy drinking. Getting drunk temporarily relieved his loneliness, but the subsequent mental anguish only increased the following day. He'd promised himself that he would never again visit the Sunlight Club. It didn't take long for his willpower to fade.

Arriving in the Dockland area for the first time in years, Frank was shocked by the damage the war had caused, with bombed-out sites littering the landscape. Miraculously, the Sunlight Club and the adjacent building had been spared. Frank wondered if any of the girls who'd worked there previously were still around. He didn't recognize the first two performers. When the third appeared, Frank found himself staring at her in disbelief.

Throughout the following day, Frank had trouble concentrating. His mind kept flashing back to the image of Penny performing on stage. She looked a little older, but she still had those beautiful, long, shapely legs and the curvy figure he remembered so well. He knew that reigniting his old habits was not a good idea. In a matter of days, he succumbed.

* * * *

Originally, Len Chatfield had sent his nephew to London for purely selfish reasons. He'd assumed the home base would recover and Frank's efforts were simply to help out in the short term. This didn't turn out to be the case. Over the years, it became clear that the company's ongoing success was almost entirely due to Frank. This irked Len, and his resentment grew steadily. He looked forward to the day he could settle the score. He hadn't anticipated the unlikely way such an opportunity would arise.

[handwritten annotation: Uncle Len resentful of nephew — Frank's success? Sacked!]

"It looks like everything is in good order," Len told his accountant at the monthly financial review meeting.

"Yes, sir; the profit percentage is within the range we projected."

"Are there any line items that have varied significantly?"

"I've only noticed one. Entertainment expenses for the London office have increased by 40% since last year."

Len knew this could easily be justified by the new work Frank had brought in since war ended. However, he sensed a possibility to embarrass his nephew—or perhaps do even more than that. Len sought the services of a private detective. He briefed the individual, giving specific areas of expenses that had caught his attention. Unaware of the surveillance taking place, Frank was an easy target; it being common local knowledge why a man would visit the second floor of the Sunlight Club.

Early one morning, Frank heard an unexpected knock on his office door. He opened it to find two men standing there. "Allow me to introduce myself," the gentleman in the black, pin-striped suit said. "My name is Godfrey Stack, of Stack and Hills Solicitors. Our practice has been retained by Mr. Len Chatfield." He pulled a letter from his briefcase and placed it on Frank's desk. "This is Bill Williams, a security guard." He said, pointing at the muscular individual next to him. "Please take the time to read the letter. If you like, I can summarize it for you. Your employment is terminated immediately, and you have twenty minutes to collect your belongings and vacate the property."

Mechanical

* * * *

Jolted by his abrupt eviction, Frank Ward spent two miserable days alone in his flat. He wasn't sure what to do, certain that returning home would be a trying experience. Though he hadn't expected a warm welcome, he was still shocked at the clinical way events unfolded. The lock on his front door had been changed, so he rang the bell. Moments later the letter box flap opened and his wife shouted through it. "I've already filed for divorce. Your mother asked me to remind you that your ownership in this house was contingent on you being faithful."

Arriving at his parents' home, his mother opened the door. "Francis Ward. You are a disgrace to our family and no longer welcome here," she said without emotion.

Back in his flat, Frank spent the entire day in bed, agonizing over his situation. He knew he was responsible for what had happened, even if it did seem a little unfair. Finally, he faced the facts and set about seeking other employment, only to find one thing he hadn't bargained for. Every potential employer required a reference from a previous employer. He'd only worked for one firm, and he knew that asking them to oblige would be futile.

With his cash savings rapidly running thin, Frank's desperation grew daily. Slowly losing the ability to reason logically, he got a welcome break when he received a telegram from his Aunty Karen. She had always been labelled the black sheep of the family, and she wasn't above using the odd cuss word—something Frank's parents thought to be quite disgusting. In his youth, Frank visited with his aunt regularly. Her telegram said she'd heard about his situation and invited him to spend time at her home.

The stay turned out to be all that Frank could have hoped for and more. He was welcomed in the normal manner. There were no words of criticism, only support and encouragement. His spirits rejuvenated quickly.

Returning to his flat in Battersea, Frank was re-energized. His focus was on finding a job. He also wanted to bring closure on a chapter in his past.

Entering the room where Penny was waiting for him, he said, "I've grown very fond of you over the years. If we'd met in different circumstances, I think we could have been friends—or perhaps even more. Life doesn't always unfold the way one would like it to. I don't expect we'll ever meet again, but I'll never forget you. I believe I've come to terms with my drinking problem and hope to set a better course for my future."

"What are you going to do now then?" Penny asked.

"I'm looking for a job. I'd like a management position in a construction firm. In the meantime, I'll take almost anything. Hopefully, I'll eventually get the chance to rebuild my career."

"You are the most unusual person I've ever met in this business and that's saying something. I never judge customers and consciously avoid anything resembling a relationship. All things considered, you are one of the better ones."

Outside, Frank climbed into the taxi. He glanced around to take one last look at the club, leaving behind him an episode in his life that had provided mixed emotions.

*   *   *   *

Arriving home one evening, Frank was disappointed to find yet another rejection letter waiting for him. He sat in the armchair, deep in thought. Yes, he would have to start considering more junior positions or perhaps another industry. Trying to imagine how he would adapt to such possibilities, his thoughts were interrupted when his phone rang. Five minutes later, he replaced the receiver, shaking his head in astonishment.

CHAPTER 9

Frank Ward arose early on Monday morning. He was scheduled to meet Alan Taylor in an East End café at eight o'clock. The previous week had produced an unexpected introduction, which resulted in him agreeing to terms for employment in Alan's new venture. He'd judged Alan to be a little rough and possibly untrustworthy, but the opportunity provided much-needed income and a chance to build a new resume.

The taxi delivered Frank to his meeting place at seven-forty. His thoughts turned to Penny Trent as he sipped a mug of steaming tea. He wondered what her relationship with Alan really was. She'd said he was a relative of a friend. He suspected there was more to it than that. He had promised himself never to visit the Sunlight Club again, but now he wanted to thank Penny in person. Perhaps he wanted more than that. He wasn't sure. There was no need for him to rush. He had more important things on his plate at the moment.

His mind was still on Penny when Alan Taylor came barging through the café door. Frank expected that they would discuss the launching of the new enterprise over breakfast. Alan's opening statement took him by surprise, "Let's go. I've got what you said you needed. I want you to check it out."

After agreeing to employment terms with Frank the previous week, Alan made another deal with the owner of a warehouse that sold building supplies. He'd be allowed free use of a small room furnished with two desks and a telephone. In exchange, he promised to purchase materials from the warehouse when projects were secured. "You told me we needed an office; now we've got one," Alan said, pointing around the four walls. "And you'll need this," he added, handing over a brass Yale key. "I'll leave you to get things set up. I'm off to a meeting. I'll see you back here on Wednesday afternoon."

Over the next two days, Frank set about establishing procedures and checking on the availability of tradesmen and subcontractors he'd worked with in the past. At two o'clock on Wednesday afternoon, Alan arrived carrying a roll of drawings. "All yours, Frank," he said, tossing the documents on the desk. "It's an extension to the council's storage facility. The bid is due at nine o'clock next Tuesday morning. I'll meet you here on Monday to see what you've come up with."

Reappearing on Monday afternoon, Alan found Frank at his desk, surrounded with drawings and calculations. "So, what have you got for me?" he asked.

"Here's the summary. Attached are details of material quantities and estimated labor costs, trade by trade.

Some prices I got from suppliers and others from subcontractors."

Alan perused the information carefully, working his way down to the total at the bottom of the third page.

"Do you have any questions?" Frank asked. He doubted that Alan understood much of his work.

"Not really. I know where we can buy bricks cheaper than your estimate. We can also do better deals on roofing and excavation. Still, that will only work to our advantage."

Frank made a mental note to never again underestimate his new boss. "Talking of that, you need to decide how much profit to include. Then I can finalize the bid."

"What's typical for a job like this?"

"Somewhere between eight and ten percent is normal. You might want to consider something lower. Winning this project would help us get off the ground."

Alan opened his briefcase. "Let's do this." He said, pulling out four standard council bid forms. "Fill in one with twelve percent profit, one with eight, one with four, and one with two. I'll think about it overnight and decide which one to deliver in the morning."

"All right, that will only take a few minutes."

"And something else," Alan added, passing over another bid form. "Just complete the necessary information on this one and leave the price blank. If I change my mind, I'll fill in another number."

At four o'clock the following afternoon, Alan arrived to find Frank busily writing letters announcing the formation of the company. "We need to get letter heading and a typewriter. I know you're trying to keep our costs down, but it will make us look more professional."

"I agree. And now you have an opportunity to make the money to pay for them," Alan responded, a sly grin appearing on his face.

"Are you hiding good news by any chance?"

"Not hiding it Frank, I'm announcing it! Hurry up, and finish what you're doing. We've got to meet the council representative at five-thirty."

"So we got the job?" Frank asked. "By the way, which price did you finally submit?"

"You'll find out soon enough."

Arriving at the local bar, Alan requested a private booth. Minutes later, the council purchasing officer joined them. "Congratulations on winning your first contract," Tom Bishop said.

"Thanks, Tom. What would you like to drink?"

"Gin tonic, please, and here's the signed agreement," he said, handing Alan a sealed white envelope.

The three men chatted amiably, though Frank was anxious to know the details of what had just transpired. "Fancy another one, Tom?" Alan asked.

"No thanks, I have to get going. We'll talk again soon," he said, giving a thumb's up on his way out.

"Come on, spill the beans. Which bid did you submit?" Frank asked the moment Tom disappeared.

A wry smile crossed Alan's face. "All five of them," he answered, tearing open the white envelope. "Let's see which one was the winner."

"This isn't one of the numbers I filled in," Frank said, pointing to the contract amount on the front page. "It must be the one you completed. Why is it typed? I didn't know you had a typewriter."

"I don't," Alan replied. "But Tom does."

Frank's face turned ashen. "I think we may have just broken the law," he whispered.

Alan grinned. "What do you mean, 'we'. The only signature I see on the bid is yours."

For several months, Frank had controlled his drinking. When Alan asked if he'd like another, he ordered a double scotch.

* * * *

Work on the storage facility got under way the following week. Frank hired a site foreman, produced a schedule, and placed orders with subcontractors and material suppliers. Alan kept a careful eye on the proceedings. It didn't take him long to see that Frank had everything under control. His only participation was negotiating discounts—a skill he'd been honing for years.

Construction of the storage facility was nearing completion and on schedule. Pleased with the performance, the council purchasing officer awarded Taylor Construction another project: repairing council flats that had been damaged by fire. He was able to do this without taking other bids because it came under the heading of "emergency situations." To get things moving quickly, the contract form was "cost of work plus a fee for profit." Frank procured bids and wrote subcontracts, and in the process, he noticed that Alan hadn't tried to negotiate discounts. He assumed that because the client was paying the cost, Alan had no incentive to reduce it. The situation was clarified for him at project completion, when subcontractor's hand-delivered envelopes filled with cash.

* * * *

While Alan's unethical behavior made Frank uncomfortable on occasion, all-in-all, he was happier than he'd been in a long time. The business was going smoothly, money was coming in regularly, and for the first time in months, he awoke every morning without a sense of nagging anxiety. All that was missing, he decided, was someone to share his life with. His thoughts turned to Penny. He wanted to thank her for helping him find employment. The next time he found himself in the dockland area, he stopped off at the Sunlight Club to deliver a note. It contained a message of thanks and an invitation to dinner. It was largely a goodwill offering, and he didn't expect to receive a response. To his surprise and great joy, a reply arrived several days later.

The following weekend, he met up with Penny at a local restaurant. The evening couldn't have gone any better. Seeing her again in a soft green dress and fetching little hat, he knew a casual onlooker would never have guessed her profession. Over a lengthy dinner, Frank learned that Penny read a lot and he was amazed at the breadth of her knowledge. When he dropped her back at her flat, she thanked him for a pleasant evening. His instincts told him not to rush things. "I also enjoyed it. Perhaps we could do it again sometime?"

"Perhaps," Penny said with a smile. It wasn't the answer he'd hoped for. Still, it left the door open.

* * * *

With several projects underway, the office needs of Taylor Construction increased, and Frank recommended they hire a typist. Alan agreed and placed an advertisement in the local tobacconist's shop window. Four women applied for the position, and the following week they were called for an interview. Frank favored Mabel, an experienced woman with strong typing skills. Alan dismissed the endorsement and settled on Margaret Brown, a pretty young girl. Frank was surprised, thinking Margaret a bit scattered and insecure. As usual, Alan was adamant.

"Look, I want someone who does what I tell them to do. The woman you liked seemed full of herself. We don't need that. In any event, Margaret had some other assets I think our friends at the council will appreciate. Two large ones if I'm not mistaken."

* * * *

Feeling his outing with Penny had gone quite well, Frank called on her again two weeks later. He was delighted that she was agreeable to another evening out. At the conclusion of an enjoyable dinner Frank asked if she'd like to go to the cinema the following Saturday "I would, Frank. But we need to be clear on one thing—I only want us to be friends, nothing more than that."

* * * *

Frank had been having the occasional date with Penny for three months before she introduced him to Daisy. He'd seen her perform on stage in the past, although they'd never spoken. In an impromptu moment, he suggested the three of them go out together. Penny was comfortable with the idea. Daisy reacted differently. "Three's a crowd, and in any case, I'll only get in the way." Eventually, at Penny's insistence, Daisy reluctantly agreed. Frank had only intended this to be a one-time gesture. The evening turned out to be so much fun that it soon became a regular event.

* * * *

With Christmas approaching, the council works manager invited the Taylor Construction staff to join his for an evening at the local pub. Alan, Frank, and Margaret attended, and at the finish of the festivities, Alan offered Margaret a ride home.

"I enjoyed the evening. I must admit, though, I assumed we'd be fed. I don't know about you Alan, but I'm starving."

"Yes I'm hungry too. I know a café that stays open late. We could stop there and get something, if you want."

"I've got a better idea. Why don't you come back to my place, and I'll cook egg and chips."

Alan cocked his head to one side and smiled, "I don't think your husband would be too pleased to see me at this time of night."

"Not to worry; he's away up north and won't be home for another two days."

Back at Margaret's home, she told Alan a little about her husband while she was cooking. They'd met in their final year at school and married three years later. She admitted that getting away from her parents was an incentive. "But he's a hardworking man who takes good care of me," she said, though even to her own ears it sounded like very weak praise. She blushed when Alan gave her a knowing look.

"What does he do for a living?"

"He's a long-distance lorry driver. Most weeks he's away for three or four nights. Would you like a drink? I've got beer, or I could make a pot of tea."

"Beer would work well," Alan said.

Margaret brought in their meals and joined Alan at the dining table. She was conscious of him looking her over and felt a pang of guilt when she realized she was enjoying the attention. She found herself comparing Alan to her husband, a kind and gentle man whom she trusted. She was certain that Alan didn't have these attributes. But there was something about his raw masculinity that aroused her.

"It's time for me to get going," Alan said, wiping his mouth on his sleeve when he'd swallowed the last remaining chip on his plate.

"No need to rush," Margaret said, hoping Alan would stay a little longer. It never crossed her mind that he wouldn't end up leaving until the following morning.

* * * *

With the bustle of New Year celebrations completed, Frank invited Penny and Daisy to join him for a traditional Sunday roast lunch. Conversation over their meal was lively, and Frank enjoyed the rapport between the two women—often pointed, sometimes racy, but clearly with underlying kindness and mutual respect. The subject of Alan was rarely raised. Frank had become aware of Daisy's sensitivity toward her son, something Penny had mentioned to him.

Dessert had just been served when suddenly Daisy started gasping for breath. With the help of a waiter, Penny led Daisy into the office where she sat in an armchair to rest.

"How do you feel?" Penny asked. She handed Daisy a glass of water.

"It's nothing. I just came over a little faint, that's all."

Back at their flat, Penny made tea for Frank and suggested Daisy take a nap.

"That's not the first time this has happened, Frank," Penny said when Daisy closed her bedroom door.

"She should see a doctor."

"I know, but she refuses too. Daisy can be very stubborn."

"What do you think's wrong with her?"

"What do you think's wrong with her?" Penny burst out. "You've seen the way she drinks, and she's constantly taking uppers to keep her energized, and those other damn pills if she wants to sleep. She's been killing herself for twenty years, and there's not a bloody thing any of us can do about it." She paused and shook her head from side to side, "Honestly, I don't know what's going to become of her."

* * * *

Margaret had been waiting for Alan to visit the office for the last two days. She asked Frank if he knew the schedule. "He rarely tells me his whereabouts. I do know he's meeting someone here at six-thirty this evening."

Alan was surprised to find Margaret still sitting at her desk. "Forgotten the time," he said sarcastically.

"I'm still here because we need to talk."

"Make it quick then. I have a visitor arriving soon."

"Look, it's important. If you don't have enough time now, perhaps we could meet later this evening. If you come by the house, I'll cook dinner for you."

Alan grinned, "Is your husband away again?"

"Yes, he's gone 'til the weekend."

"All right, I'll be there around eight-thirty," he replied, recalling his last memorable visit.

Margaret placed two plates of bacon, chips, and baked beans on the dining table, then took the seat opposite Alan's.

"How have you been?" he asked, enjoying a home-cooked dinner he'd seldom eaten since leaving his mother's house.

Margaret put down her knife and fork, and a solemn look replaced the previous smile.

"I have something serious to tell you."

"Well, get on with it then," he said, cramming another helping of bacon into his mouth.

Softly, she said, "I'm in the family way."

"That's not serious, Margaret; it's something to be happy about. Congratulations! Are you hoping for a boy or a girl?"

"No, you don't understand. You see, you're the father."

Alan swallowed slowly. "Don't be ridiculous, you're married. Next you'll be telling me you never have sex with your husband."

"It's not like that. Yes, of course I do, but we made a pact before we got married. He wanted us to save so we could buy a little cottage in the countryside and then start a family."

"Let me get this straight. You admit to having sex with your husband. Now, you're trying to convince me that I'm the baker who put a bun in your oven. What is this, Margaret? Are you trying to blackmail me or something?" he said, raising his voice.

"I'm not blaming you, Alan. My husband—well, I don't want to go into details. Let's just say he's extremely careful. I'll have to tell him sooner or later, and I'm sure he's going to think I've been unfaithful."

"I'm not buying this old bag of bollocks," Alan shouted. "Look, I don't believe for one minute it's my baby. If you think it is, then you should have an abortion."

"I could never do that. It's against my beliefs."

"Fuck your beliefs. Now I know you're just trying to screw money out of me."

"How could you!" Margaret responded, for the first time visibly showing her anger. "Look, I admit sleeping with you of my own free will. At the same time, you didn't object, did you? Try behaving like a man and accept responsibility for your behavior."

Alan thought quickly. He decided to hedge his bets. "I'm not admitting to anything. If you're just looking for money, I may be willing to come to an arrangement. Of course, we'd have to have an agreement that this matter remains strictly between the two of us. And if I do give you a settlement, I'd have no further obligations."

"First off, I need to try and convince my husband it's his baby. If I'm able to do that, some cash would come in handy. But Alan, don't you dare imply this tragic situation is only about money. That's extremely cruel and inconsiderate."

"Let me know what happens, and we'll try to work something out," Alan said coldly, walking swiftly to the door.

* * * *

The manager ran into the dressing room, startling those performers sitting inside. "Quick, all of you, I need your help," he called out.

"What's wrong?" the new girl asked, unsettled by the troubled look on the manager's face.

"It's Daisy—she collapsed at the end of her routine."

The girls rushed to help while the manager scampered upstairs to call an ambulance. Ten minutes later, the paramedics arrived to find Daisy covered with a blanket and her head supported by a makeshift pillow. They checked to ensure she had a pulse, before carefully lifting her onto a stretcher. Throughout the proceedings, Penny was in a trance, staring vacantly at Daisy's limp body. "The show must go on," the manager said with the noise of a siren reverberating in the background. But the mood had turned sour, and the normal banter was replaced by eerie silence.

Penny finished her last act in a daze. She rushed to the bathroom, removed her makeup, changed into street clothes, and set off to the hospital. Upon her arrival, she explained her relationship with Daisy to the receptionist. Two hours sitting in the waiting room passed slowly, and with each minute, Penny's anxiety increased.

Eventually a nurse appeared, "Miss Penny Trent?" she asked.

"That's me," Penny replied.

"Come with me, please. I'm taking you to a private office. The physician who attended to Daisy will be along shortly."

Several minutes later, an elderly man with grey hair and large black-rimmed glasses arrived, "Hello, my dear," he said softly. "I understand you are Daisy's friend and flat mate."

"That's right; how's she doing?" Penny asked, praying for the answer she so desperately wanted to hear.

The doctor removed his glasses and let out a sigh. He'd only said the words "I regret to tell you," when Penny fell to her knees sobbing. "No, no. Please tell me it isn't true. Not Daisy. Not my dear, dear, Daisy. Not the only true friend I've ever had. Surely life cannot be so cruel. Oh my God. I can't believe it."

The doctor helped Penny back to her feet and took her in his arms. "It's always hard losing someone you love. Things may seem very bleak at this moment. Sometime in the future your friend will be a fond memory." Penny wasn't sure if she had or wanted a future without Daisy.

CHAPTER 10

Wilson Plumbing had been in business for seventeen years, eight of those under the leadership of George Lambert. While market demand fluctuated, growth had been consistent, both in scope and geographical location. Initially, the firm focused on small repair and maintenance projects, rarely venturing more than ten miles from home base. Over the years, George enlarged the firm's capabilities. In addition to drainage and water lines, they were now installing bathroom and kitchen plumbing, together with ventilation and heating systems. With projects becoming larger and more complex, they expanded their territory, operating both in the county of Essex and Greater London.

George derived much satisfaction from his firm's success, but family was always his number-one priority. He knew how lucky he'd been to meet Lilly, and adored his daughter, Rita, who'd just turned thirty-five. Though she'd never fully recovered from the loss of her husband, she remained a kind-hearted and devoted mother. George's granddaughter, Kate, was approaching her fourteenth birthday, and remained a constant source of joy. She was an excellent student who'd passed the Eleven Plus exams, a prerequisite to attending grammar school. She also pursued healthy activities and had many friends, which made George proud. Most of all, he loved the fact she'd never lost the caring qualities apparent since her formative years.

In the early days of Henry Wilsons' retirement, his wife's health remained stable. They travelled to all the places they'd dreamed about, and Henry had become optimistic about the future. Unfortunately, his hopes were to be dashed. Following a trip to Cornwall, Susan fell into a coma and passed away peacefully a few weeks later. George and Lilly attended the funeral, and while Henry seemed at ease, his disposition reflected a deep inner sadness. They hoped and prayed he would be able to find other interests to help him heal from his great loss.

Four months passed before George set eyes on Henry again. The change that had taken place was difficult for him to believe. He'd lost a great deal of weight, making his face gaunt and wrinkled. Six months later, George received a telegram, advising that his friend and mentor, Henry Wilson, had died. The doctor determined death was from a cold that turned to pneumonia. George and Lilly were certain their dear friend had died from grief. When Henry's will was disclosed, he'd left all his shares in the business to the Lambert's.

* * * *

In response to Wilson Plumbing's expansion, George re-structured its management, and he met regularly with each of his key personnel. First thing on a Monday morning, he allotted time with Arthur Thomas, his estimating manager. Their agenda consisted largely of reviewing opportunities and determining which ones they would pursue. When they'd finished running through the weekly list, Arthur said, "And George, if you haven't already seen this, I'm sure it's something you'll be interested in." He handed over an article he'd cut out of the morning paper. "I believe it's located in your old stomping ground."

George put on his glasses, and moments later his face lit up. The snipping from the business page read:

> *Council decides to move forward with the Crescent Street Project. The proposed scheme calls for the demolition of three hundred dilapidated terraced homes. They will be replaced with high rise towers containing 900 modern flats, a school, shops, a church, and 500 underground parking spaces.*

"It's about time," George said, looking back up at Arthur. "Those homes are in terrible condition. The government should be ashamed of themselves for allowing people to live there all these years."

George's mind started wandering. "Despite the decrepit state of the neighborhood, Crescent Street brings back many fond memories." He closed his eyes as events from his childhood came flashing back. "I know I shouldn't be sentimental in business matters, Arthur, but I really, really, want to get this job. Find out all you can about the council's plans, and I'll visit a few of my contacts in the area. We'll meet again next Monday to discuss a winning strategy."

CHAPTER 11

Alan Taylor and Frank Ward had always been an unlikely duo. Frank would have most certainly chosen another job if he'd had viable options at the time. Despite their differences and the tension these sometimes caused, they proved to be an effective team. Frank was an exceptional organizer and a natural leader who related well to staff and clients. Though Alan seldom adhered to the 'Queensberry Rules' he had an uncanny knack of finding opportunities, negotiating deals, settling disputes, and enhancing profits.

The company earned its stripes by completing several small projects for local councils and this led them to larger opportunities. Through these, Alan got to learn about "ringing," a method utilized by contractors bidding for local authority construction work. Contrary to intent, there was no real competition; the contractors met beforehand in private to predetermine who would get the award and the bid price. To ensure the process looked authentic, the balance of competitors submitted a bid a little higher than the established winning one.

Though strictly illegal, this practice was unlikely to raise suspicion because all bids were thinly spread. Even if the authorities suspected the procedure was rigged, it was virtually impossible to prove; it would require a self-incriminating confession. Most participants recognized the benefits as each would get their turn to win a project with a high profit margin. Participating in the ring, Alan soon emerged as its acknowledged leader, for on occasion a new contractor to the scene refused to participate. Invariably, a meeting with Alan would cause them to change their minds.

With larger projects under its belt, Taylor Construction relocated into modern offices, and within a decade of starting operations, they had become one of the premiere contractors in the region.

Business success allowed Alan to live in the manner he'd always dreamed about. With ready access to cash, he led the high life and made sure all those around him were fully aware of it. He joined exclusive clubs, rented a penthouse apartment, drove a luxury car, and wore tailored suits. He also entertained lavishly; partly to attract potential clients, also to showcase his wealth and influence.

On a personal front, there was no shortage of women. Having the God-given gift of being six-foot three, with masculine features and money to spend, many females were easy pickings. While Alan liked to arrive at public events with a good-looking chick in tow, he had no desire to develop a lasting relationship. His interest in attractive women was simply to make him look successful and satisfy his lust.

* * * *

With continuing growth, Alan saw no limits to his potential. An evening conversation with Tom Bishop, the council purchasing manager, caused him to reflect. "Cheers," Tom said, taking the first sip of his second pint.

"Cheers, Tom. When you called earlier, I got the impression there was something on your mind?"

"Look," Tom said abruptly. He put down his glass and his manner became earnest. "You and I have been friends for many years, and it's worked well for both of us." He began to tap his fingers on the table, uneasy with what he had to say next. "But you need to be careful. I've heard several rumors recently, both from inside the council and from subcontractors. Let me just say they weren't very complimentary."

Alan paused and his eyes narrowed. "Tell me more."

"Well, most people in construction get some bad knocks whether they deserve it or not. You've got to counterpunch and offset negative rumors with good press. I know a bloke in public relations who may be able to help. We've used him at the council to deal with potential scandals, and he's very good. Not only that, but he's one of us, if you know what I mean."

* * * *

At first glance, Alan was wary of Jimmy Dickson's clean-cut looks and demeanor. His concern subsided when Jimmy spoke. "How's it going, mate?" he asked in a gravelly cockney accent, which put Alan more at ease.

Over a lengthy lunch, washed down with a bottle of French merlot, Alan listened carefully to his guest's advice and suggestions, chiming in every so often to seek clarification.

"Let me sum it up, Alan. You need to get a better image. I can introduce you to two newspaper reporters. Both of them can get articles printed in the local rags if you treat them right."

Alan paused, looking Jimmy up and down. He wanted to make sure he was to be trusted. "What might that involve?"

"Dinner at nice restaurants and the odd football match. And of course they both like to help maintain the world's oldest profession, especially if they're not paying." Jimmy grinned. "Of course, we need to find the right subjects for them to write about. Charities normally do the trick. I can get you a list of entities council members support and others that always go down well with the public at large. Last of all, we need to work on your image within the industry."

Alan's mind was racing, "Spit it out then."

"First, you need to improve working conditions. Or at least give that impression," he turned his head sideways and winked. "Both the press and the public, lap up stories about happy workers. I'm sure we could find a way to arrange that. Then, we need to find subcontractors who'll say the right things. I'm certain you have some ideas, and I'll help to make that happen."

"Jimmy, we need to discuss the details. In general terms, I like what I hear."

"If you hire me, I'll help iron everything out."

"The one thing we haven't spoken about is money," Alan said, speculating what this might cost.

"I believe in giving value, so here's my proposition. I'll make the necessary introductions and provide appropriate information. I'll meet with you regularly for the next six months to make sure you get results. In return, I'd like you to build a bedroom extension on my house. If you're still happy with me at the end of my assignment, my missus and I would enjoy a holiday in Spain. That way I have an incentive. No money changes hands, and you have tax write-offs."

Alan stood up and shook Jimmy's hand. "I like the way you think."

* * * *

"Here's the morning paper, sir," Alan's secretary said, placing the tabloid alongside the incoming correspondence. Normally, Alan turned directly to the sports section. Today, the headline of an article grabbed his attention.

Council Votes to Proceed with the Crescent Street Project

Alan's mind drifted back to his youth. Crescent Street was his childhood home, and he still knew people in the area. He started to imagine what a sweet triumph it would be, to become a hero in his old neighborhood where people had looked down on him and his mother. Securing the project would be a huge challenge. He knew his company had the capability, and he may be able to use his influence with local contacts. Alan was still consumed with the subject when noon came around "I'll bloody well show them," his secretary overheard her boss mutter as he left for his lunch appointment.

CHAPTER 12

"Good morning," Tom Bishop said, sure he knew the reason for Alan's call. Later that evening at Tom's local, Alan asked if he'd any ideas that might help him secure the Crescent Street Project.

"I'm afraid not. It's by far the biggest undertaking in the council's history. Everyone will be watching it like a hawk. And there'll be no funny business. I've already heard that all interested parties will have to sign under oath that they've not collaborated or conferred with any other firm."

Alan had been hoping for more. "When will it go out to bid?" he asked.

"It's hard to say. The council's having conceptual sketches prepared for public discussion. Then the drawings need to be completed. I think it will be another year before its bid. That gives you plenty of time to prepare."

* * * *

At their quarterly meeting, John Ball, the solicitor for Taylor Construction, pulled Alan aside. "I wanted to talk about the Crescent Street Project. I mentioned your interest to my partner, and he has an idea. Perhaps we could discuss it over lunch this Thursday."

John was waiting to greet Alan in the reception area at the Worthington Club. He escorted him to a private dining room where he introduced his partner, Bruce Babcock. Bruce had been briefed on Alan's personality. He quickly got down to business. "Mr. Taylor, during the war I worked for the London County Council. My main responsibility was the preparation of contracts for construction projects. Because many were extremely urgent, we developed a design-build contract and legislation was rushed through to allow its implementation. This method gave the contractor full control, which in turn produced faster delivery of projects." He looked carefully at Alan, trying to gauge his reaction. It also provided John the opportunity to chime in, and he seized the moment. Peering over the top of his half-moon glasses he said, "We've researched the matter. While this method hasn't been used since war ended, the legislation has never been repealed."

Alan raised his eyebrows as he listened. He didn't fully understand all the nuances, but his gut told him the concept had potential. "Tell me more about design-build."

"Basically, the council provides conceptual drawings, quality requirements, and other pertinent criteria. The contractor employs his own architect and assumes full responsibility for design and construction of the project. Some think it increases the contractor's risk. If properly managed, I think the reverse could be true. Also, it tends to limit competition."

Bruce allowed Alan time to absorb the information.

"How do they select the contractor?" Alan asked.

"It's a combination of things. Price, schedule, and the firm's experience are normally the key factors. John tells me you may have influence with certain council staff. Of course we're not suggesting anything improper. However, if they did take this approach—"

Alan interrupted, "No need to elaborate," He said, his mind already racing with possibilities. Without saying another word, he shoveled down the remainder of his lunch and took off, leaving his hosts to finish their meals alone.

* * * *

Alan sat at his desk deliberating the meeting with his solicitors'. The possibility of winning a huge project with limited competition made him salivate. He knew it would take the votes of four council members to adopt a design-build approach. He also knew that was unlikely unless he could exert some influence. His mind went into overdrive, thinking through a variety of tactics that he may be able to employ. Despite knowing it would surely be an uphill battle, the prospect of making it happen captivated him.

To get matters started, he arranged a meeting with Tom Bishop, who was able to provide general information on all the current councilors. Armed with this, he and Bruce Babcock invited members Stevens and Evans for lunch, two councilors who always voted along similar lines. The topic posed to entice them to attend was, "How could Taylor Construction help charities in their jurisdiction?" a subject that Jimmy Dickson, his new P.R. man, thought would likely grab their attention.

Following the usual pleasantries, Alan mentioned his interest in helping handicapped youth. Councilor Evans' confirmed that supporting unfortunate children was a worthy cause. Stevens' reacted with little enthusiasm. This didn't faze Alan. He knew that Stevens' wife was the treasurer of a home for disadvantaged children and would be careful to avoid any perceived conflict of interest.

At a break in the group's conversation, Alan casually asked about progress on the Crescent Street Project. Both Councilors confirmed that things were moving ahead and expressed their strong support for affordable housing. Alan had expected Bruce to raise the subject of project delivery at this juncture. To his annoyance, Bruce appeared to ignore the opportunity. Bruce, however, was a wily individual. During his days at the council, he'd learned the importance of timing. With lunch coming to an end, he cleared his throat, a technique he'd perfected to draw attention. "Councilors, unquestionably members of your ward would greatly benefit if the Crescent Street Project could be delivered at record pace. Clearly, there is a tremendous need. In these inflationary times, faster completion would also save money." He paused, giving his audience time to reflect. "During the war it was essential to get projects completed at record speed. To accomplish this, we adopted a design-build contract. There's no doubt in my mind that projects could still be delivered this way. It would, of course, require strong and imaginative leadership."

Neither of the councilors' commented. Their facial reactions told Bruce all he wanted to know.

* * * *

One week later, Bruce Babcock called Alan to inform him that he'd received a call from the council purchasing department. They'd invited Bruce to visit in order to learn more about the contracting methods used during the war. Encouraged by this news, Alan arranged a get-together with Joe Richards. Joe had been the council's timekeeper on Alan's first project in the haulage business. One of Joe's co-workers, Peter Downs, had recently been elected onto the council.

"Do you still keep in touch with Peter?" Alan asked, returning from the bar with two beers.

"Occasionally, we get together and reminisce."

"Has his elevated status changed him at all?" Alan asked with a grin.

"He probably talks a good game with others. I know too much about his past for him to pull the wool over my eyes." The two men laughed. "Those were the days," Alan said, hoping Joe would think he'd changed his ways.

"Don't give me all that old nonsense. Next you'll be trying to convince me you attend church every Sunday," Joe said, causing Alan to adopt a wry smile.

"I suppose we were all a bunch of scallywags in those days. It didn't really hurt anyone, did it?" Joe asked, not expecting an answer.

"You're right," Alan said. "Changing subjects, have you been following the news regarding the Crescent Street Project?"

"Of course, and it's about time, if you ask me. I assume you must be interested. It would be a feather in your cap, especially being a local."

"Well, I've been thinking about it. There's bound to be a lot of competition, so I've not made my mind up yet."

"I see your point. It's a pity there's no way the council could give preference to locals; that would make sense."

Seeing the opening, Alan asked, "Just hypothetically Joe, if they did, do you think Peter Downs would support me?"

"No doubt about it, particularly if I reminded him of his timekeeper days," he said, turning his head and winking.

Comfortable he'd achieved his objective, Alan bought more drinks, and they spent the balance of the evening discussing football.

* * * *

Bruce Babcock called Alan to provide an update on his meeting with the council purchasing department manager. "He asked a lot of detailed questions and took copious notes. It was obvious he'd been asked to provide a detailed report. He also happened to mention that his research was being carried out at the request of Councilors Stevens and Evans."

The following day, Alan received a call from The Spencer School for Children with Special Needs. "Good morning Mr. Taylor. I understand your company may have an interest in supporting our mission. Perhaps you'd like to meet with Mrs. Linda Stevens. She's a board member and our treasurer."

* * * *

When Alan stepped out from his maroon Jaguar, he was approached by a distinguished looking woman wearing a fur wrap. "Good morning, you must be Mr. Taylor."

"Mrs. Stevens?"

"Yes, and thank you for responding so quickly," she said with a smile.

Mrs. Stevens took Alan on a tour of the facilities, pointing out maintenance issues and other shortcomings. Afterward, she invited him to join her for tea in the canteen.

"Well, Mr. Taylor, I'm sure you can see why we're so desperate for donations. Most of the children who reside here have already experienced enough challenges. We're committed to making things comfortable for them. Of course, it takes money."

Alan bowed his head slightly, "Please, call me Alan. Yes, the need is very clear. I greatly admire the wonderful work you're doing. It would be an honor for my company to make a contribution."

"Why, thank you, Alan," Mrs. Stevens said, blushing slightly. "Every penny helps."

"I think we can do better than that, Mrs. Stevens."

"Please, Linda," she said, her eyes glistening.

"Well, we'll certainly take care of all the repairs. And I'm pretty sure we can renovate or replace the faulty equipment," he said, with a frown of concern.

"Why Alan, that's more than I could have possibly hoped for," she said, taking his hands in hers and smiling serenely.

"Leave it with me. I'll get in touch with your caretaker, and we'll schedule the work at the earliest possible time."

"Thank you again, Alan," said Mrs. Stevens, fighting back tears while escorting her visitor to his car. "And if there is ever anything my husband and I can do for you, please, just let me know."

Alan drove away basking in the knowledge that once again he'd outwitted someone he considered a privileged, stuck-up old cow—and in the process she was actually crying with gratitude.

* * * *

Despite the progress he'd made, Alan knew he needed at least one more vote for the council to approve a design-build approach. He'd run out of ideas to use guile or gentle persuasion. He knew he had to engage other tactics. To determine his course of action, he met with Jimmy Dickson, who'd already earned his holiday in Spain. True to form, Jimmy provided personal information on the other four council members, and this led Alan to conclude that councilor Jack Phillips was probably his best bet. Apparently, Jack thought life had dealt him a bad hand; he'd not done well in his career, and his marriage was shaky. He liked to be entertained, because this fed his weak ego. The driving force behind his political ambitions was to improve his social standing and get the respect he thought he deserved. Due to an unhappy home life, he also enjoyed the company of women, though he'd never done well in that area, either.

Alan picked up the phone. "Frank, can you join me for a moment? I have a little job for you."

"How can I help?" Frank asked when he arrived at Alan's desk.

"I want you to entertain Councilor Phillips. Invite him to the next home game at Upton Park, and take him to dinner afterward—I think that's right up his street."

"Has this anything to do with the Crescent Street Project by chance?"

"You don't need to worry about that. Just make sure he enjoys himself."

"Well, that doesn't sound too difficult. But I've a feeling you're up to something."

"Oh, and Frank, another guest will be joining you."

"Who's that?"

"Her name is Christine Morgan. She's an old acquaintance of mine."

"I've not heard you mention her before. What does she do?"

"She used to be a typist. Now she cares for older people. And Frank, at the appropriate moment I'd like you to leave, so Christine and Councilor Phillips can spend some time alone."

Frank frowned. "Now I know you're up to something."

"Not me Frank, honestly," Alan said, raising both his arms in the air and pulling a face. "It's just that Christine would like to get to know the Councilor."

Not for the first time, Frank took off, shaking his head.

* * * *

At two o'clock on Saturday afternoon, Frank met Jack Phillips in the parking lot outside West Ham United's home turf, and escorted him to their reserved seats. They'd been discussing the team's season when a pretty young girl with blonde hair tied back in a ponytail arrived. "Hello, I'm Christine Morgan", she said, taking the empty seat next to Jack's. "I'm a friend of Alan Taylor."

Jack pretended to be interested in the game. In truth he was preoccupied, eyeing up Christine's shapely figure whenever he thought she wouldn't notice. At the game's conclusion Frank escorted his guests to a restaurant that enjoyed a reputation for serving some of the best steaks in London.

Over dinner, Jack tried hard to find an accord with Christine and in the process discovered their mutual interest in history. At a break in the conversation, Frank glanced at his watch. "Goodness, I didn't realize the time. I'm sorry, but I have another engagement to get to. I'll take care of the bill. You two can stay as long as you like," he said, thanking his guests for their attendance and saying final goodbyes.

Terry Bush

Jack was excited at the unexpected chance to be alone with Christine. He hoped she'd stay long enough for him to get to know more about her. "Are you in a hurry? If not, maybe you'd like another glass of wine?"

Christine smiled, "My last bus doesn't leave for another forty minutes. But I think I've had enough to drink, thank you."

"Rather than bother with public transport, I could drive you home if you wish."

"That's very kind. I wouldn't want to inconvenience you, but if it doesn't put you out, I'd be grateful for a ride."

Jack's interest in Christine had started the moment he set eyes on her. She was much younger than him and that may be an obstacle to seeing her again. He knew he didn't have much time, so he decided to find out more about her personal situation. "Do you have a boyfriend?" He asked casually.

"I have a few male acquaintances. Nothing serious," Christine replied.

Emboldened by the response, Jack weighed up the pros and cons of asking her out. In the process of doing so, Christine said, "Wow, look at the time; I think we should be getting on our way."

Jack was sure he'd been too forward and that his obvious interest had not been well received. He was disappointed at the way a promising evening was winding up. The drive to Christine's flat only took ten minutes and there was little conversation during the journey. Not expecting anything more than a polite farewell, he was pleasantly surprised when Christine said. "It was nice to meet you. I appreciate the ride home. Do you have time for a cup of coffee?"

Christine made their drinks, placed them on the small table and sat in the chair opposite Jack. Their conversation returned to the subject of history, and Jack silently vowed not to ask any further personal questions, instead, build on what they had in common. At a break in their discussion, Christine yawned, which Jack took as a signal for him to leave. He was juggling with the idea of suggesting another get-together, when Christine asked, "Jack, judging by your ring, I assume you're married. You haven't mentioned your wife all evening. Are you by chance in an unhappy relationship?"

"You're very observant. And unfortunately, correct. My wife and I haven't been close for a long time."

Christine's expression changed from a smile to a look of sympathy. "That's very sad. Maybe I should try to cheer you up," she said as she placed herself on Jack's lap.

* * * *

At first, Jack wondered if he'd been dreaming. When he rolled over and saw Christine's naked body, memories of what had taken place earlier came rushing to his mind. He looked at his watch. It was two-thirty in the morning. His thoughts turned to the excuse he'd give his wife for being so late. He climbed out of bed quietly, not wanting to wake the beautiful young woman he planned on seeing again. He dressed quickly, scribbled his office phone number on a sheet of paper, and left it on the bedside table.

* * * *

"Hello Alan, its Bruce Babcock," the voice at the other end of the line said. "I thought you'd like to know I've been asked by councilors Evans and Stevens to prepare a report on the pros and cons of the design-build method. They're going to put the matter on the agenda for the next monthly meeting."

"That's good news, Bruce."

"It's encouraging. Unfortunately, the feedback I'm getting indicates that they may not have enough support."

"How short are they?"

"I think there's one more member they can convince, but it appears that the other four are opposed."

"Keep me posted," Alan said.

Not wanting to draw attention to himself or his company, Alan asked Bruce Babcock to attend the next council meeting and report back. "Usual posturing," was Bruce's summation. "Mind you, I think Stevens and Evans are only using the subject for political reasons. Apparently, Councilor Downs is also in favor—something I have the feeling you may have helped with," Bruce said, giving Alan a knowing look. "As for the others, well, they're all cowards when it comes to doing anything out of the ordinary. I hate to say this, but frankly, I think getting a positive vote looks unlikely."

Bruce expected Alan to be angry, knowing how badly he wanted the design-build method to be adopted. To his surprise he remained calm. "We'll see," was the casual response.

* * * *

"I need you to take councilor Phillips out again," Alan told Frank.

"What's it this time?"

"Actually, Frank, your previous guess was correct. It does have something to do with Crescent Street."

"So, what is it you want me to do?"

"Simple. Persuade him to vote in favor of adopting a design-build method."

"It sounds like he's totally against it. That being the case, how do you expect me to change his mind?"

"You're a very persuasive person Frank. However, if he proves to be difficult, I think these will help him see the light." Alan removed a red box and a white envelope from his desk drawer and handed them to Frank. "Why don't you take these back to your office and then figure out what you're going to do."

Twenty minutes later, Frank reappeared; he was red in the face. "Fuck me, Alan. You're going to get us both locked up one day!"

"You worry too much. Let me know how it goes."

* * * *

When Jack Phillips arrived at the Limestone Club, he was shown to a private room where Frank Ward and Robert Davis were waiting for him. Robert had been hired by Alan several years previously. Now, he was one of the firm's senior managers. At first Frank had been skeptical of Alan's choice. Robert turned out to be competent and, as Alan had pointed out on many occasions, "He understands the real world, does what he's told, and knows when to keep his mouth shut."

The three men ordered *hors d'oeuvres* and engaged in topical conversation. When the main course arrived, Frank changed subjects. "How are things going with the Crescent Street Project? And do you think the council will approve the design-build approach?"

Jack hadn't heard Frank mention the project previously. He assumed it to be a question of general interest. Because this wasn't a subject he wished to discuss, he made his answer deliberately vague. "Well, I believe the matter has been raised."

"And where do you stand on it?" Frank asked.

Jack Phillips was normally a passive individual. He could, however, be obstinate if he felt someone was leaning on him, "I think the council will do what it always does," he said in a tone indicating a general lack of interest.

"You may know that Mr. Taylor was born in Crescent Street," Frank said. "He believes the local community will benefit if the project is built and delivered quickly, irrespective of whether or not Taylor Construction is involved."

Jack Phillips put two and two together, realizing the football match and tonight's dinner amounted to nothing more than trying to win his favor. "If Taylor Construction is interested, they'll be able to submit a bid at the appropriate time."

Robert topped up the councilor's wine. "Mr. Phillips, I think Mr. Ward and Mr. Taylor are keen to get your support. They both believe it's best for the local people."

Councilor Phillips was now seething. He didn't know who'd started the discussions about design-build. He wasn't sure how it might benefit Taylor Construction, but clearly they were pushing the issue against his wishes. "Gentlemen, perhaps there's a misunderstanding here this evening." While he still wanted things to end on a harmonious note, he intended to make his point clear. "I've enjoyed getting to know you and trust we can continue our new-found friendship. I also hope you'll bid on the Crescent Street Project. I have a duty to do what I think's right for the residents in our district. I believe they are best served by bidding the Crescent Street Project in open competition. That's my final position on the matter. I suggest we move on to other subjects."

Jack sat back in his chair. He was pleased with himself, thinking he'd been decisive and had put the matter to rest. The conversation moved on to other subjects. When the waiter arrived to collect their empty plates, Frank asked him to hold the desserts for fifteen minutes.

Robert refilled the wine glasses. Then he removed a box from under his chair and placed it on the dining table. Jack was puzzled by what was happening. He wondered if the box contained a gift. If that turned out to be the case, he would leave immediately.

Frank stood up and looked at Jack. Then he put his hand inside the box, and said, "Councilor Phillips, I think you may be interested to hear this."

At first Jack could only hear muffled noises. Things soon changed. He recognized the soft melodic voice of Christine Morgan saying, "Jack darling, I find you very attractive and interesting. From the minute we left the restaurant I was hoping we'd end up making love, and now we're going to."

This was followed by the councilor's voice telling Christine she was the most beautiful girl he'd ever met, and he could hardly believe they were in bed together.

The blood started to drain from Jack Phillip's face. He realized he'd been set up, and worst of all, Christine had been an active participant. "That could be anyone's voice; you can't prove it was mine," he shouted defiantly.

Frank gave Jack a smug look. "I don't think the council members or your wife will have much trouble identifying it. Just in case they do, I think this will help clear things up." He pulled a photograph from his jacket pocket and flipped it onto the table. It didn't show Jack's face, but the tattoo on his back that he'd acquired while serving in the army was clearly visible; and with Christine's naked thighs wrapped around his waist, there could be no possible misinterpretation of what they were doing.

Any fight Jack had left in him disappeared. He sat silently like a kidnapped man dreading what his captors may do next.

"Jack, we also hope our friendship will continue." Frank said quietly as he and Robert exited the room.

* * * *

The council meeting had some heated exchanges. Finally, it just came down to a vote. Three of the councilors met in the pub afterward. They'd been certain of prevailing and were totally mystified by Councilor Phillips' last minute change of mind.

CHAPTER 13

"Would you like tea or coffee, sir?" Alan's secretary asked.

"Tea," he said, without looking up from the morning paper. "Make it two cups; Jimmy Dickson will be here any minute."

"Morning," Jimmy called out as he came bounding into the office. "Congratulations on the council's vote."

"It's a start," Alan replied, throwing the newspaper into the waste bin. "But we've still got a lot to accomplish if we're going to be successful. What news do you have for me?"

"Things are moving along quickly. A committee has been appointed to oversee the process, and they'll also evaluate the bids. That's good news being that Joe Richards is on the committee, so we should be able to get regular updates from the inside. Architects are working to produce conceptual plans, and the building department is preparing criteria for the qualification process."

"In real terms, is this all just coming down to price?"

"No it isn't. Price will be important of course, but the council members and the committee are putting a lot of emphasis on other things. If we play our cards right they should work in your favor"

"What other things?"

"Schedule is going to be a priority. There's nothing I can do to help with that, so I suggest you put your thinking cap on. But there's a great deal of importance being put on local knowledge and standing in the community. Now that's where I have some ideas, and I'm betting you do too," Jimmy said, playfully slapping Alan on the back.

* * * *

"We're putting the final touches on the bid and qualification document. It will be ready first thing tomorrow," Frank told Alan who'd said he needed ample time to review it. "It's due to be submitted by no later than five o'clock on Wednesday. That gives you almost the whole day to look it over.

"Good," Alan replied. "By the way, I intend to deliver it personally."

* * * *

At four o'clock on Wednesday, Alan got into his Jaguar and headed toward the council offices. He delivered the bid, and then headed toward the Fox and Hounds pub for his six o'clock meeting.

"How's it going?" Alan asked Joe Richards when he walked into the saloon bar.

"I'll be able to answer that better this time tomor-row," Joe said.

"So, what's the deal?"

"The bids were received this afternoon. They've been locked in a safe which will be opened at eight o'clock in the morning. At that time, the selection committee will be present, and then we're all going to a private and secure room. Lunch and refreshments will be brought in, and nobody will be allowed to leave until we've come to a decision."

"Blimey, it sounds like a trial," Alan interjected.

"You're right, it does. But the council wanted to make sure there was no outside influence, so this is the process they set up. Of course, the committee only has the authority to make a recommendation. That will have to be blessed by the council. Again, to ensure no outside interference, council members will be arriving at five o'clock to review the committee's findings and make a final decision."

"Any chance they'll question the committee's recommendation?"

"I think that's highly unlikely. They're politicians, Alan. This gives them cover and the chance to blame someone else if things go tits up," Joe said, chuckling loudly.

"Can we meet tomorrow night then?"

"Of course we can. Let's make it seven o'clock at Henry's lounge bar. It'll either be a happy or miserable occasion, I suppose. Either way, there'll still be a reason to get plastered."

"That you can bank on," Alan said, ordering another round.

*   *   *   *

Alan had been waiting in Henry's lounge bar for nearly an hour, strumming his fingers on the cocktail table with one hand, nursing a large scotch in the other. Just as he was starting to wonder if a problem had cropped up, he saw Joe coming through the front door with a face like a fiddle.

With his head bowed down, Joe said, "Bad news I'm afraid."

Alan was stunned. He'd been optimistic about his chances and hadn't expected to be disappointed. "Who got it, then?" he asked quietly.

Joe faltered. "When I say bad news, I meant for the other two bidders!" he exclaimed, noisily pulling up a chair and grinning like a Cheshire cat.

"You had me going there, you bastard!" Alan shouted, spinning Joe around and calling out, "Waiter! Get this man a very large drink!"

Finally, settling down at the table, Alan said, "Hurry up, and fill me in on the details."

"We ended up only getting three bids. Word had it we were going to get four or five. I think the article in last week's paper condemning firms alleged to have been involved in ringing may have caused some to withdraw," he said, giving Alan a sideways look.

"All three prices were close, but you scored really well on the other sections. The photo of you and Linda Stevens at the Children's Home went down well, as did the personal letters from current and former employees. However, I think the tipping point might have been your letter heading. Funny enough, I know the owner of the Ironmongers store, and I happened to bump into him last week. He told me he'd rented out the shed at the back of his shop for a hefty amount, and at the time I thought he was joking. But Alan, when the committee saw Taylor Construction's registered address as 29A Crescent Street, nearly all the council members stood up and clapped."

CHAPTER 14

Alan Taylor took his place at the head of the board room table, where Frank Ward and Ray Parker, his chief estimator, were prepared to give him an update.

Since being awarded the Crescent Street Project, they had weekly reviews, knowing the risk associated with this form of contract was different from anything they'd done previously.

"Are we on schedule? And the answer had better be yes," Alan said caustically. A large penalty clause for late completion had his full attention.

"So far, we're on track. Site offices are in place and the supervisory team's been mobilized. Demolition is underway and we should be starting excavation in two or three weeks," Frank reported.

"Good," said Alan, turning his attention to Ray. "And how's the design coming along?"

"Our architects are a little behind. As I've mentioned before, we have to check their drawings constantly to make sure they're in line with the scope and quality we've committed to. I think we knew this when we priced the job. In all honesty, I'm not sure we understood how much time and effort it would take."

"How far behind are they?" Alan asked.

"Approximately two weeks, I'd say."

Alan's eyes narrowed, "I might pay a visit to remind them who their working for."

"I'd advise you to be careful," Frank interjected. "Ray's correct. Although we knew their work needed to be carefully reviewed, none of us had any previous experience in this area. One thing's for sure. They could kill us financially if we don't keep the design in line with our budget, and that takes time."

Alan scowled and pounded his fist on the table, "I won't be dictated to by a bunch of toffee-nosed bastards who think they're better than us!"

"Look. Ray and I understand your frustration, but we've got to be practical."

"Whatever it takes, you have to find a way to get them back on track. Let me change subjects. Are they keeping in line with the budget?"

"There are a few increases in the foundation design. I think we'll be able to cover them with our contingency. We're reviewing everything with a fine-toothed comb. It's difficult to judge until each trade is finished," Ray said.

"Stay on it, and we'll continue to meet regularly until all design work is finished," Alan said, getting up, stomping across the room and slamming the door behind him.

*   *   *   *

From Frank's tone, Alan sensed something was up, "Ray's just come back from his weekly design meeting," said the somber voice on the internal phone. "I think we have a big problem on our hands."

Fifteen minutes later, Frank and Ray arrived in Alan's office. "What's the skinny?" he asked tersely.

Frank's eyelids blinked involuntarily, "I'll let Ray tell you."

"Well, the scope of the mechanical, plumbing, ventilation and drainage work has increased," Ray started out.

"I know. You told me that at our last meeting!" Alan said, raising his voice. "I also told you to make those fucking architects fix it!"

"Calm down, Alan," Frank interjected. "It's not Ray's fault, and I don't think it can be fixed. We have to face up to the fact that we didn't fully understand the implications of design-build, and we've underpriced some of the work."

Alan glared at Frank. "You'd better explain."

"Let's start with why this has happened. The bid documents contained information in the form of performance standards. We did our best to interpret them. On reflection, we should have engaged experts to help us quantify the scope. Unfortunately, there's been a knock-on effect, which has compounded the problem. Let me give you a few examples. The heating system gave a range of required room temperatures for each season. Although we thought we'd made reasonable assumptions regarding radiator sizes, boiler capacities, etc., we missed the mark. This in turn has led to coordination issues. On another matter, the bid criteria said we had to conform to published council standards. We thought we'd done our homework. It turned out that there were certain things hidden in documents we didn't even know existed."

"What documents? Give me an example." Alan barked.

"Well, all bathrooms have to include a water heater and a shower hose. That's a new one on me, and apparently it only came into force a few months prior to our bid."

"Bloody council," Alan growled. "We didn't even have a bath when I was a kid. In any event, a water heater and shower hose doesn't cost that much."

Ray felt the sweat running down the back of his shirt collar. "True, but remember we have nine hundred bathrooms."

Alan drummed his fingers on the table. "So how much extra is this all going to cost?"

We have some work to do. At a guess I'd say it'll add 35% to the mechanical and plumbing budget, and that doesn't include the corresponding delay costs.

An eerie silence followed. Alan stood up and walked slowly around the office, his hands clasped behind his back. "Look," he said. "I don't want you to mention this to anyone. I'm going to think about it, and I'll get back to you."

Left alone, Alan reflected on the probable loss he was facing. Knowing he wouldn't be able to focus on another subject, he got in his car and drove to an isolated area overlooking the river Thames. There was something about this location that had a calming effect on him. His mother had brought him here when he was young and told him stories about the river. It was an integral part of London's colorful history, and had been a focal point for the largest empire the world had ever known. Watching ships arriving from destinations far and wide had always fascinated him, and it was one of the few places where he could truly relax.

Two hours sitting on a wooden bench made Alan hungry, so he took off to a fish shop close to the flat where he was raised. The journey took him past the Crescent Street Project. He slowed down to observe the huge signs displaying the Taylor Construction name. Caught up in the moment, his angst disappeared and an idea came to mind.

*   *   *   *

The following morning, Alan arrived at the office earlier than normal. To Frank's surprise, he seemed to be in a good mood. He read his mail, and then called the partner of the architectural firm responsible for the Crescent Street Project.

"Good morning, Gerry, I'd like to visit with you. Are you free for lunch today?"

Gerry was well aware of the problem that had surfaced recently. He was also familiar with Alan's temperament and style. "Of course, does my club at noon work for you?"------- He asked his secretary to cancel his existing lunch appointment when Alan hung up.

* * * *

Gerry had been waiting patiently for Alan to raise the issue he'd spent the entire morning mulling over. He was confident that his firm had no liability. He didn't think that would hold much water with Alan, so he prepared himself for the expected onslaught. While dessert was being served, Alan asked casually, "When will the mechanical and plumbing drawings be finished?"

Gerry's face began to twitch, "Next Wednesday. I understand the situation for you is serious, and I'm very sorry. I know that doesn't make things any better, but the root of the problem stems back to the interpretation of the council's documents—prior to our involvement."

Alan stared at Gerry with half-closed eyes. "This is what I want you to do. I'll collect the drawings personally next Wednesday. I don't want you to tell anyone. And I mean anyone."

Gerry wasn't sure how to respond; the directive seemed bizarre.

"Is that clear?" asked Alan, raising his voice a notch.

"Eh, well, yes, I suppose so," Gerry mumbled, trying to make sense out of the situation.

"Don't you dare let me down," Alan growled, slowly closing the distance between his host's face and his own.

Gerry began to perspire, "Of course not," he replied, his voice trembling.

Back in his office, Alan phoned Dick Casey, the deputy chief estimator. In corporate matters, Dick was conservative and generally considered to be a 'yes man.' On a personal level, he had the reputation of being a womanizer.

"How can I help?" Dick asked cautiously. He'd seldom met with Alan alone.

"Dick, I'm considering placing the mechanical and plumbing contract with the Wilson Company. In addition to submitting the lowest bid, I have reason to believe the firm's owner will be especially cooperative. That being said, we've never worked with them. I want you to visit their office and report back your findings."

"Is there anything in particular you want me to look at?" Dick asked.

"Just the usual; meet their estimator, get a sense of their organization and anything else you think relevant."

"All right, I'll get straight to it."

"And one other thing, find out who Miss Telford is." Alan said, pointing at the signature on the confirmation of drawings receipt attached to their bid.

On Wednesday morning, Alan Taylor drove to the architect's office and collected the drawings Gerry had promised. His visit was brief and his only words were, "Remember, I don't want anyone to know these have been issued until I tell you otherwise."

Later in the day, he phoned Wilson Plumbing. "Good afternoon, Mr. Taylor," George Lambert said courteously when his receptionist transferred the call.

"Please, call me Alan. We've never met, although I've heard a lot about you. I understand we were born in the same street, so I'm sure we've got a lot in common."

"How can we be of service?"

"I'll come straight to the point, George. We'd like to talk with you about the Crescent Street Project. Are you available on Monday morning?"

George was shaking with anticipation. A visit from Dick Casey the previous week had been encouraging, and now a personal invitation from Alan Taylor made him believe that securing the project was a real possibility. "Certainly," he replied, "Is there anything I should bring with me or prepare for?"

"Just bring your estimator and the bid. Then we can talk turkey. Does nine-thirty work for you?"

"We'll be there sharp," George said, wishing Alan goodbye and hanging up.

On Friday morning, Alan told Frank about the meeting he'd arranged with George Lambert. "Wouldn't it be better to wait for the revised drawings to arrive? I think that might improve our negotiating position" Frank said.

Alan shrugged, "Let's see how Monday unfolds first." While Frank knew they needed to make a commitment in the near future, he was concerned that they may be jumping the gun. He'd learned over the years to only give advice if it was clear that Alan's mind was made up. Once alone, Alan called Dick Casey, "What time are you leaving the office today?" he asked.

"Usual, around five-thirty," Dick said.

"Stop by and see me when you're ready to go."

At five-forty, Dick knocked on Alan's door. "You wanted to see me?"

"Yes, there's something I want you to do," he said, getting out of his chair and picking up the roll of drawings sitting on the coffee table.

"I want you to deliver these to Wilson Plumbing's office first thing Monday morning. You told me they open at eight-forty-five, so you'll be able to get back here by ten o'clock at the latest. Make sure you get the pink drawing receipts Miss Telford issues and bring them directly to my office. And Dick, one last thing—I don't want you to tell anyone about this, not now and not ever."

Dick was troubled. He'd always been intimidated by Alan. For reasons he didn't understand, the current instruction made him nervous.

Relishing Dick's discomfort, Alan added for good measure, "That's quite clear Dick, isn't it? I wouldn't want you to forget."

"Absolutely," Dick said, feeling his heart beat faster. "You can be certain this will stay strictly between the two of us."

Alan contemplated his upcoming meeting with Wilson Plumbing. He'd been digging around for information on George Lambert's background. He found character traits' that he could likely exploit. George was honest and trustworthy.

CHAPTER 15

Had a good day dear?" Lilly asked when George arrived home Friday evening.

George beamed. "Yes, I'm meeting with Alan Taylor on Monday morning. It sounds like he's interested in making a deal on the Crescent Street project."

Lilly threw her arms around her husband, "Oh George, how wonderful! I'll be thinking positive thoughts, and I'm sure things will work out for you."

* * * *

George woke early on Monday morning and he was raring to go. Sensing her husband's excitement, Lilly got up to cook his favorite breakfast—fried eggs and bacon with toast—knowing this would give him a good start to his important day. By seven-thirty, George was ready to leave. He'd arranged to pick up Arthur Thomas at eight-fifteen. It was only a twenty-minute drive, so he decided to take the longer scenic route to help pass the time.

Driving slowly down the country lanes, George reflected on his life. Now fifty-seven years old, he felt he'd had an amazing journey. His mind returned to days at the market. Happy times he thought, particularly working alongside his dad. He couldn't possibly have imagined what lay ahead. Meeting Lilly and then Henry Wilson, he believed he'd led a charmed life.

Seeing Arthur's house in the distance, George realized he'd been day dreaming; He had no recollection of his surroundings since crossing the bridge five miles back.

"Good morning," said Arthur, who was waiting at the curbside. "Did you have a good weekend?"

"Grand, thank you," George said, smiling at his young employee. "Perhaps, today will be even better."

On their journey, George told Arthur he expected they'd be asked to reduce their price. "I'll handle that," He said, "if it's more than I'm prepared to accept, we'll discuss it in private before I give a final answer."

"If you don't mind me asking, how much lower are you willing to go?"

George had total trust in Arthur, and was comfortable sharing confidential information. "If push comes to shove, I'll knock off five percent. In theory, that would make our profit margin very thin. It wouldn't worry me though. Given the scale of work, I'm confident we can improve productivity." George thought about his answer, and found himself listening to Henry Wilson's voice echoing in his mind. "Never forget, George—you must always be firm when you've reached the bottom line. Go any lower, and you'll live to regret it." George smiled to himself, knowing Henry would be pleased with the opportunity that lay ahead.

The traffic was light, and at nine-fifteen, they pulled into Taylor Construction's parking lot. Alan Taylor's secretary was waiting to greet them in the reception area. She escorted them to the meeting room on the sixth floor where she offered tea or coffee. On the stroke of nine-thirty, Alan Taylor arrived, accompanied by Frank Ward.

"George, it's great to finally meet you," Alan said, introducing Frank and acknowledging Arthur. "I've only ever heard good things about you and your company. Perhaps fate intended two local boys like us to work together."

"You may be right," George said, surprised by such friendly opening comments. He'd heard about Alan's reputation of being a tough individual. Seeing him in person reminded him of several locals he'd known in the neighborhood when he was a child. His instincts told him to be careful.

"You and I know the construction business, and we're both familiar with the Crescent Street area. I'm not going to screw around, and I'll just come straight to the point."

George was wondering what Alan's point would be.

"This project is going to be a huge challenge, and we want the best trade contractors possible. We've considered our options and think you're a great choice. Naturally, there's always the question of price."

"What do you have in mind?" George asked, not wanting to fall into the age-old trap of lowering the bar.

"Simple. If you reduce your price by four percent, we can sign the contract today." Alan pulled two copies of an agreement from his briefcase and placed them in front of George.

"Would you like the opportunity to discuss my offer alone?" Alan asked, sensing George's hesitation.

Inwardly, George was bubbling over. "If you could give us a few minutes, I'd appreciate that," he said calmly. He didn't want to show his hand too quickly.

"No rush. Why don't you review the proposed terms of agreement at the same time? If you're happy with them and agree on the price, we can sign it right here and now," Alan said, leaving the room with Frank in tow.

George relaxed for the first time since arriving, "I think we're there," he told Arthur, "I didn't want to seem too anxious to make a deal; it could set the wrong precedent. Of course, I'm going to accept his offer. Now, let's review the terms to make sure we're happy with them."

Twenty-five minutes later, Alan tapped on the meeting room door. "Are you ready for us yet, or would you like a little longer?"

George looked up, "We're all set. We've decided to accept a four-percent reduction. Naturally this trims our margin. If we work closely together, I think we can improve productivity. That would work to our mutual interest."

"You can count on it," Alan said, "Did you review the agreement?"

"Yes, its industry standard. We have no issues. The schedule's correct. Our drawing receipts that form part of the agreement are stapled to the back. All that remains is to insert the revised price. We believe this is the new number." George said, handing over their calculations for a four-percent reduction.

With the number already committed to memory, Alan just glanced at the document. "Dead on," he said, leaning across the table and shaking George's hand. "So, let's get matters concluded." He picked up the phone and dialed his secretary.

"How can I be of assistance, sir?" Miss Potts asked, appearing through the meeting room door moments later.

"I'd like you to type a price on the front page of each of these two contracts," he said, pointing to the appropriate lines. "Here's the new number." He handed over Arthur's calculation sheet. "Bring them back when you've finished."

To fill in time, Alan asked George how he got into the plumbing business. George had only just started to explain how he'd met Henry Wilson when Miss Potts returned with the two contracts.

"I'll finish that story another time," George said. "I think we have more important things to attend to."

Alan placed the contracts on the table and pulled a gold fountain pen from his inside jacket pocket. "Gentle-men, will you please do the honors?" he asked, addressing George and Frank. "Could you sign the signature block on the front page, and date and initial the bottom right hand corner of all the others. George, being our guest, it would be appropriate for you to go first."

George was overcome with excitement. He had difficulty keeping his hand steady working his way through each page. When Frank had completed the same exercise, Alan leaned across the table and shook George's hand again. "Welcome on board. Now it's time to get to work," he placed one copy of the contract into a white envelope and passed it to George.

"We're delighted," George said, allowing himself to smile for the first time. "When do you want us to get started?"

"Frank will be in touch with you shortly to finalize those arrangements."

Once settled in the privacy of his car, George let out a whoop of delight, startling Arthur, who'd never seen him react that way. On the drive back they talked in great detail about the preparations needed. Arthur assumed, that caught up in the moment, George hadn't noticed he'd just sailed past the office. He was about to mention it when George braked and pulled up outside the Coach and Horses pub.

"I've always avoided a lunch time drink on a work day," George said, "Today's going to be an exception."

They feasted on ham and egg pies and toasted the Crescent Street project several times with best bitter.

"See you tomorrow, and thanks for all your help," George said, dropping Arthur off outside his home.

Lilly spent the entire day praying her husband's important meeting had gone well. She readied herself for his arrival. When George came crashing through the front door the look on his face didn't require explanation. He threw his briefcase onto the settee and took hold of Lilly's hands. Together, they danced a jig last performed at their wedding reception.

CHAPTER 16

Arthur Thomas arrived at the office early on Tuesday morning, still on a high from the previous day. He was running behind schedule and needed to focus on a bid for a school extension that had to be delivered the following day. George turned his attention toward assessing availability of staff and the best choices for the Crescent Street Project.

With the school bid off his plate, Arthur worked his way through two days of correspondence, phone messages, and new drawings. One of these caught his eye: updated drawings for the Crescent Street Project, something he mentioned to George later in the day. "Not surprised," George said. "The set we bid on had many details missing. I expect this fills them in."

"That probably means we have some change orders," Arthur said.

"More than likely I suppose. If possible, I'd like to avoid asking for extra money at this early stage in the proceedings. Take a look at them when you get the opportunity and let me know. If they're really small, maybe we'll try to absorb them."

"I should have time tomorrow. That being the case, we can discuss the subject at our Monday review meeting," Arthur replied.

* * * *

At ten o'clock on Monday morning, George joined Arthur in the meeting room. "Good morning. How was your weekend?"

Arthur looked up from his pile of notes, his eyes were glazed, "I'm sorry," he mumbled, "What did you say?"

George looked closely at his estimator, "Are you all right? You look exhausted."

Arthur gathered himself. "Actually, I didn't get much rest. I started looking at the latest Crescent Street drawings on Friday afternoon. It didn't take long to realize the extent of the changes. Knowing you'd want the details, I spent the weekend doing a comparison with the bid set. Here's the summary," he said, handing over his report.

When George finished reading Arthur's findings, his mouth was wide open. "Good heavens. I'm sure Taylor Construction included a contingency. Though I doubt they anticipated anything like this."

"I have to agree. With this quantity of changes, I'm surprised they didn't call us to explore possible alternatives," Arthur said.

George looked pensive. "I've a feeling Alan Taylor is a crafty man. Perhaps he thought with an agreement signed, they could lean heavily on us in the process of negotiating change orders. If that's their game, they won't find me rolling over."

"Is it possible they just haven't realized the implications?" Arthur asked.

"You may have a point," George said, clasping his hands together and looking skywards. "We tend to assume large contractors have good procedures. Over the years we've often found to the contrary. I think we should hold tight for a few days. If we don't hear from them this week, I'll follow up to make sure they're prepared for what's coming."

* * * *

Frank Ward had spent two days puzzling over Alan's last minute decision to finalize a contract with Wilson Plumbing. He'd just received the updated drawings so he decided to approach Alan on the subject. "I wanted to talk about last Monday's meeting. I must say, you caught me completely off guard."

"Why's that?" Alan replied nonchalantly.

"Well, knowing the magnitude of changes coming, I thought you'd wait for Wilson to price them and negotiate from there."

"No need to, everything is taken care of."

Frank began to wonder if his boss had grasped the severity of the matter. He took a deep breath, "Sorry, I'm not following you."

Alan pulled the signed agreement from his drawer and tossed it on the desk. He looked down his nose and said, "I think you'll find this covers everything."

Frank looked at the agreement he'd signed two days previously. He frowned. "This contract is based on the bid set drawings. The latest drawings have just arrived and they contain numerous increases."

Alan turned to the last page. "If you look carefully, you'll find this receipt includes the latest drawings."

Deep furrows formed on Frank's brow. *Had Alan truly misunderstood the contract that had been signed?* Meanwhile, Alan was enjoying Frank's obvious confusion. With a grin on his face he pointed to the date on the drawing receipt. Then he stared at Frank. Slowly the penny dropped. "Oh, my good God!" he bellowed. "You switched the bloody form, didn't you? How on earth did you get the receipt in the first place?"

"We have a signed agreement based on the current drawings. That's all you need to know."

Frank swallowed, "I'm not sure how you did it, but it sounds like fraud to me."

"If two competent companies willingly enter into a contract, it's not fraud. In any event, you might do well to remember who signed it," Alan said, leaning back in his chair and clasping his hands behind his head.

Frank's face went pale, and he whispered, "I'm sure we'll hear from them when they find out what's happened."

"I've no doubt. All you need to tell them was we didn't force them to sign anything. They'll be serious consequences if they don't meet their obligations."

* * * *

"Heard anything further from Taylor Construction?" Arthur asked at their weekly meeting.

"Funny, I was about to ask you the same question. It's difficult to believe they're still unaware of all the changes. If I don't hear from them this morning, I'll call to get clarification."

Shortly after returning from lunch Arthur's phone rang. "It's George. Could you come to my office and bring the Crescent Street agreement with you?"

Arthur thought George looked anxious, "Is there a problem?" he asked cautiously.

"I'm not sure," George said, relaying details of the conversation he'd had with Frank Ward a few minutes earlier.

Arthur listened carefully. "To be honest, I don't understand. He's saying our bid includes the updated drawings. That doesn't make sense."

"I agree, and all the terms were standard. Unless…" George paused, "they rewrote something that we missed."

"I don't think that's possible. It's the standard printed agreement. We would have noticed if they tried to alter the wording or slide something in."

"Arthur, you went to college and studied contracts. I'd like you to read it again and make sure. Then I'll call Frank Ward back and tell him he's got it wrong."

"No problem. It's only five pages; I can double-check quickly."

George watched nervously as Arthur carefully reviewed the document. When he finished reading the last page, he looked up, "There's nothing in here that suggests we absorb changes. It's either a try-on, or maybe they still don't understand the new scope. We're clearly covered; our price is based on the drawings we had at the time. They're listed on the drawings receipt stapled to the agreement," Arthur added, sure this would put his boss at ease.

"Thank you," George said, exhaling deeply and leaning back in his chair.

Arthur was about to return to his office when something caught his eye. "Jesus Christ!" he shouted.

"What is it, Arthur? What's the matter?"

Arthur collected himself, "I've just noticed something—the pink receipt details the latest drawings, not the ones our bid was based on!"

George looked puzzled. He picked up the agreement, put on his glasses and read the receipt. He looked up at Arthur and muttered, "How could this possibly be?"

Both men were silent as they tried to figure out what could have taken place. George spoke first. "The date on these drawings is the same day we signed the contract. What time were they delivered to our office?"

"I'll ask Miss Telford," Arthur said, picking up the internal phone. "Around 8.45 a.m. Dick Casey delivered them in person."

George ran through the sequence of events at their Monday meeting, two weeks prior. Suddenly, something sprang to mind, "Arthur, we both read the agreement. I don't think there's any doubt the bid set receipt was attached to it. However, do you recall that Alan Taylor had his secretary take the documents to her office, in order to type in the revised price?"

"Of course," he said. "They must have switched the form at that time." With his worse fears confirmed, George went red in the face, "The two-faced conniving bastards," he said bitterly. "I'm not going to let them get away with this."

CHAPTER 17

"It's clear you've been hoodwinked. The challenge will be to prove intentional deceit," Walter said, upon hearing George's story.

Walter Simpson had been the company solicitor since Henry Wilson first started his car repair shop. Now in his seventies, his two sons managed the business, allowing him to serve only long- standing clients whose company he enjoyed.

"Does that sound practical?" George asked.

"The problem is that it may come down to their word against yours. They will undoubtedly say there was an open negotiation. That you had time to review the contract and willingly signed it. I've no doubt the receipt was switched. The problem is, how are we going to prove it?"

"Won't they be under oath?"

"If we can get this into a courtroom, they will be. Even that doesn't guarantee the outcome you're looking for. People like Alan Taylor are willing to lie. And you can be sure he's already covered his tracks with anyone else who was involved."

George sighed aloud, "What do you suggest?"

"I'd like to think it over. Are you available for lunch on Thursday?"

* * * *

The doorman greeted George and accompanied him to the table where Walter Simpson was halfway through his second gin and tonic. Walter outlined his review, "There's no doubt the contract price is based on the drawing receipt form, which you initialed and dated. For a judge to take the case, you'll have to convince him you couldn't reasonably have known you were signing the incorrect receipt."

"What do you think the chances of that are?" George asked.

"That's hard to say. He may agree to a preliminary investigation. Then we'd have to come up with some hard evidence. Hearsay won't do it, and it's highly improbable we'll get a confession from Alan Taylor or Frank Ward. Additionally, if other staff were peripherally involved, they were almost certainly unaware of what was taking place."

George groaned, "I realize I'm up against a devious man, and yes, I suppose I should have taken greater care. But he's the crook, not me. My main concern now is to protect the financial interests of my family."

"If you complete the contract without receiving additional compensation, what do you think will be the outcome?"

"Not good I suspect. Maybe we can improve efficiency; if not, it could wipe me out."

"Not good options. I don't wish to be overly pessimistic. I should warn you about the other possible consequences of proceeding with a law suit. It will undoubtedly take a lot of time and be a huge distraction—something you've never experienced. I did a little background checking. Apparently, disputes are nothing new for Alan Taylor. From what I can gather, he normally prevails. In addition, he has strong connections with the press. I can almost see the headlines now—Wilson Plumbing signs contract and then refuses to honor it. I suggest we both think things over and meet again next week."

"All right," George said quietly. "Let's keep this to ourselves. I'd hate for Lilly to find out. She'd worry herself to death."

* * * *

Wilson Plumbing had been working on the Crescent Street Project for eight months. George met regularly with his accountant to carefully review the financial situation. The losses were starting to mount up, necessitating the transfer of funds from the investment account into working capital. One morning, George answered his phone. On hearing the distinctive Old-Etonian accent, he didn't need to ask who is was, or why he was calling.

"Hello, George, it's Peter Bradley. It's been a while; are you available for lunch this week, old chap?"

In the diplomatic fashion George had come to expect, the bank's branch manager waited for coffee to be served,

"We've noticed that you've withdrawn most of your savings over the last several months."

George hesitated. While he wanted to protect his interests, he didn't want to mislead a long-standing friend, "Yes, the Crescent Street Project has proved to be a bigger challenge than expected. I'm optimistic the worst is behind us."

"I'm pleased to hear that, old boy, I really am. Unfortunately, and, regretfully, we will probably need to cut back on your line of credit."

George had hoped to avoid this additional setback, or at the very least, delay it, "What exactly will that involve?" he asked.

Hoping he could avoid the impression of a personal involvement, Peter said, "The overdraft committee will review the situation and let you know."

The following week George met with his accountant to analyze the impact of the letter that had just arrived. For several months, he'd been praying he could make it through the Crescent Street Project, and then rebuild. Now, with the credit line effectively removed, he knew that was no longer possible. Unable to concentrate, George sought solitude to assess his situation. He drove into the local countryside and parked in a deserted layby. He closed his eyes and reflected on the wonderful times spent in the area with Rita and Kate. Slowly, his thoughts drifted back to his present predicament.

He knew he'd been in denial, and that his focus should now be solely on protecting his family.

* * * *

"Things may not be all bad," Walter Simpson said when George updated him on the latest news. "You've got the house and the mortgage is paid off. You own the office building and workshop. I recommend you sell them quickly and deposit the proceeds in an account for Lilly. There's nothing improper about that; you haven't yet filed for bankruptcy. I would also suggest you transfer the ownership of the two company cars into Lilly's name." Walter gave a wry smile. He badly wanted to help his client see things in the best light possible. "Rita still works, and Kate's growing up. I think you'll get by without much of a problem. And remember—you're only fifty-eight. With your experience, you'd have no problem finding a job if you needed to."

George was grateful for Walter's advice. He only wished he could show more enthusiasm. While he understood certain things could be salvaged, he still felt like a total failure. "Can I make those arrangements discreetly through your office?" He asked.

"Most certainly you can. I know an honorable estate agent who will handle it confidentially. You'll need to give me power of attorney. If you come by my office tomorrow, I'll have the necessary forms ready for you to sign."

* * * *

While George knew he'd done everything possible, he couldn't prevent his mood from darkening. Hiding it soon became his biggest challenge. Minimizing interaction with staff, and adopting a 'stiff upper lip' when necessary, was manageable. Trying to replicate that at home was a different kettle of fish. No matter how hard he tried, Lilly increasingly asked, "You don't seem your normal self, my darling. Is everything okay?" He attempted to blame his demeanor on a variety of reasons; in his heart he knew Lilly wasn't convinced.

One more meeting with his accountant confirmed the firms' resources would only cover the next payroll. Seeing no good reason to delay further, George decided it was time to break the news. In recent years, Arthur Thomas had become his confidante. He decided to tell Arthur over lunch, and inform the rest of the staff the following day.

Arriving in separate cars at a village pub, George ordered drinks and ham rolls, allowing Arthur to find a table where they could talk in private. George put on his bravest face and with a quivering voice he said, "It's been a wonderful journey, and I appreciate all you've done for me. Regrettably, it's come to an end. Our losses on the Crescent Street Project have depleted our resources. In other words, Arthur, we're bankrupt."

Arthur had never seen George looking defeated; it made him uncomfortable and sad. "I'm terribly sorry to hear this, George, and I'm certain it's entirely due to that cheating bastard, Alan Taylor. One day, he'll get his comeuppance and so he bloody well should. My wife and I will always be grateful for the wonderful opportunity you gave us. I truly hope things work out well for you and your family."

"At the end of the day, Arthur, I only have myself to blame. I wanted you to be the first to know. I'll be informing the rest of the staff tomorrow."

"If you don't mind me asking, how is Lilly bearing up?"

"I haven't told her yet; I didn't want her to worry. I'll let her know when I've informed the staff. I'm praying she's not going to be upset with me for her being the last to know."

"I doubt there's ever a good time for such things," Arthur said with his eyes welling, "I'm certain Lilly will understand."

George noticed Arthur's discomfort, and, forever considerate, he told him to take off whenever he wanted. Arthur was grateful for George's thoughtfulness. He decided to exit tactfully. George didn't want to go back to the office, and getting home early would only promote unwanted questions. He decided to go for a drive. He'd just placed his empty glass on the counter when he felt a tap on his shoulder. He looked around and saw Ben Morrison, a retired banker from his neighborhood. "Fancy seeing you here George, I didn't know this was one of your haunts."

"Actually, it's my first time," George said, "a colleague recommended it, so I thought I'd give it a try."

"What would you like to drink? I'm sure I must owe you one."

Normally, George limited himself to one pint if he was driving. Given the circumstances, another seemed like a good idea. Seeing that George was alone, Ben introduced him to two of his friends. The four men engaged in lively conversation, touching on cricket, fishing, and the upcoming local elections. At a break in the conversation, Ben light-heartedly suggested it was George's round. Enjoying the camaraderie and rationalizing that he wasn't far from home, George obliged. With the consumption of more alcohol, the conversation turned to storytelling. Most ditties had been repeated numerous times in the past. That didn't prevent the inevitable laughter, which in turn led to another round of drinks.

When the final bell rang, George had temporarily forgotten his troubles. He was about to take off when Ben asked, "Would you like to join us for a game of cribbage? The publican is a good friend of ours. He lets us stay on after closing time if we wish."

George stopped to think. He was certainly in no rush, and he'd enjoyed playing dominoes in his youth. It would also give him the opportunity to clear his head. Upon the departure of the last patron, each participant drew seven pieces, and Ben set up the cribbage board in order to keep score. At the conclusion of the first set, Tom, a retired farmer, opened his bag and took out a large flask of whiskey together with four glasses.

* * * *

The game finished at four o'clock; as had the contents of Tom's flask. George thanked the group for including him in the afternoon's entertainment and took his leave through the back door. On his journey home, he started to experience spells of dizziness. At the same time, his dark mood returned. The distraction of cribbage, alcohol, and mixing with a friendly group was replaced by a feeling of despair. He was sure his family would be distraught when they found out what lay ahead. And what would Henry think if he knew what had happened to the company he'd worked so hard to build? Driving along the narrow lanes, George's frustration increased, and a myriad of thoughts flashed through his mind. *How could he have been so naïve and stupid? Didn't he know Alan Taylor's reputation? Was it just an ego trip to win the Crescent Street Project rather than following sound business practice? How could his family possibly forgive him? And furthermore, why should they? You've really screwed things up, George, and you've only yourself to blame. Now you have nothing to look forward to—nothing at all.* Accelerating rapidly down Apple Hill, George started to lose focus and he squeezed the steering wheel so tightly that his fingers began to go numb.

* * * *

When Lilly Lambert answered a knock on her front door, she was surprised to find Jim Robinson standing there. Jim was the local Chief Inspector of Police, a fellow member of the parish advisory committee, and a family friend.

"This is an unexpected pleasure. Won't you come in?" Lilly asked, leading Jim into the living room without waiting for his reply. "I'll put the kettle on," she said, smiling to herself. Jim always teased her about the obsession she had with making tea for visitors.

"Lilly, before you do that, please sit down for a minute. I have something I must tell you." He readied himself. "A short while ago, we received a call from a motorist who'd seen flames coming from the woods at the bottom of Apple Hill. He stopped to investigate and found they were coming from a car that had crashed into a tree. Lilly, it was George's car. I'm so terribly sorry to tell you this. George was killed in the crash."

Lilly stood up and clutched her chair. She couldn't comprehend Jim's words. Surely there had been some mistake. Not George, not the kind, loving man who'd always taken care of her. Lilly looked at Jim, hoping something would change. The tears forming in his eyes confirmed her worst fears. Lilly felt faint and she started to lose her balance. Jim managed to catch her and help her back onto a chair. He struggled for the appropriate words, "Can I make you some tea, Lilly?"

Lilly sat in silence while Jim held her hands. Even in her pain, she remained polite, "Thank you, Jim. Kate and Rita will be home soon. If you don't mind, I'd like to be alone for a while."

"I understand," Jim replied, feeling helpless and inadequate. "I'll let myself out. Please call me at any time if there's anything I can do."

On hearing the front door close, Lilly burst out crying. Gathering herself, she managed to climb the stairs and go inside her bedroom. She picked up the photograph of her wedding day and kissed it tenderly. Overcome with grief, she fell onto the bed, sobbing uncontrollably.

CHAPTER 18

Sheila had been mourning her brother's death for a little more than six months. She knew that it had been a very difficult time for his wife, daughter, and granddaughter, so with her husband's concurrence she invited them all to visit for the holidays.

"Harold and I were wondering if you and the family had any plans for the Easter," Sheila asked Lilly when she answered the telephone. "If not, we thought you may like to stay with us for a few days."

"That's very kind," Lilly replied, "but we're going into the East End this weekend. My mother's not well, and we'll also be visiting George's grave."

"I understand, my dear; just thought it might give you a break."

Lilly paused for a moment. "Sheila, if it's all right with you, perhaps Kate could visit. She's taken the passing of her grandfather very badly. Given one of the reasons for our trip, I'm sure she'd prefer to spend time with you rather than accompanying Rita and myself."

"If she'd like to, we'd be delighted to have her. Harold can collect her on Saturday morning and take her back home the following Thursday."

* * * *

Kate was pleased to hear the arrangements for Easter. She enjoyed the company of her mother and grandma, but hadn't relished visiting grandpa's grave. The memory of his funeral still reduced her to tears whenever it entered her mind.

Saturday came quickly. At nine o'clock, Uncle Harold arrived and drove Kate back to his Hertfordshire home. Walking through the entrance door, Kate was immediately struck with the mouthwatering smells coming from the kitchen. Aunt Sheila was preparing chicken with roast potatoes to be followed by blackberry and apple pie, dishes she knew Kate enjoyed. Over lunch, they discussed Kate's agenda, and as always, there was a long list of activities to choose from.

Three wonderful days that included horse-back riding, making jam and taking long walks, left Kate pleasantly exhausted and ready for an early night.

"Uncle Harold will be up at the crack of dawn tomorrow," Sheila told Kate, while they were preparing supper together. "Friends from our days living in Scotland are passing by tomorrow. Your uncle is taking Mr. McKinney for a tour of the local area, and his wife, Morag, will be coming here for breakfast."

"Perhaps, I'll also get up early and pick spring flowers from the woods," Kate said. "And afterward, gather mushrooms for our lunch."

"Super idea; I'll pack a small bag with fruit and biscuits for your breakfast. You can use it to carry the mushrooms, and I'll put some string in it to tie the flowers. I'll remind your uncle to give you an early call, and I'll see you back here for lunch."

At six-thirty on Tuesday morning, Harold gently knocked on Kate's bedroom door. "Time to wake up, Kate," he whispered. "I'll see you later."

Kate got out of bed, put on her gown and tiptoed to the bathroom. She took a quick shower, got dressed, and then crept quietly down the stairs to make tea. Now ready for her morning's activities, she grabbed the packed bag that her aunt had prepared. On her way along the side passageway that led to the front garden, she felt a little light headed. She'd stayed awake longer than planned the previous evening, engrossed in the love story she was reading. Sure that closing her eyes for a few minutes would help clear her mind, she sat in the wicker chair and rested her head against the wall. She knew she shouldn't stay for too long; Aunt Sheila would be up at eight o'clock and it would be embarrassing if she'd not left after asking Uncle Harold to wake her at six-thirty.

* * * *

Waking with a start, Kate realized she'd fallen asleep. She heard voices, recognizing one of them to be Aunt Sheila's.

Judging by the Scottish accent, the other one was her aunt's friend, Morag. From the sound of china clinking, Aunt Sheila and Morag were sitting at the kitchen table drinking tea. Only the passageway wall separated them from her.

The longer Kate sat there, the easier it became to hear the conversation. She heard Morag say, "I was very sorry to hear about the tragic death of your brother."

"It was truly heartbreaking. I miss him tremendously. He was such a good man. You'll get to meet his grand-daughter later. She left early this morning to pick mush-rooms and wildflowers. She'll be back here for lunch."

Kate heard the women stirring their tea. "Morag, if I were to tell you something, would you please keep it to yourself?"

Morag raised her eyebrows. "Is it about George?"

Sheila nodded. "Yes it is."

Morag bit her lip. "You have my word. I wouldn't dream of repeating something if you didn't want me to."

"Well," Sheila began, "when I tell you what happened, you'll understand why I'd like it to stay confidential."

Sheila told Morag about her conversation with Lilly following the post mortem. She gave details of how George had been double-crossed by Alan Taylor in a business transaction on a large project in Crescent Street. This led toward Wilson Plumbing's bankruptcy, which in turn sent George into a downward spiral. Totally out of character, he'd been drinking at lunchtime, the most likely reason for his fatal accident.

At the mention of her grandpa, Kate froze, her ear pressed hard against the wall, hanging onto every word.

"You poor thing, that must have been awful for you and the rest of the family. I know stress can cause people to act in unpredictable ways. No doubt that's what happened. Were charges pressed against Alan Taylor?" Morag asked.

Kate thought she heard her aunt cry. "Lilly met with the company solicitor, and also spoke with the police. Apparently, there wasn't enough evidence to take the matter to court, so eventually it got dropped. There's no doubt in my mind, however, that slimy worm, Alan Taylor, effectively killed my brother."

With their tea finished, Sheila invited Morag to join her in the sunroom. Kate used this as her cue to slip quietly through the corridor and be on her way.

On her walk to the woods, Kate became obsessed with the words that kept echoing in her mind. *Alan Taylor killed my grandfather. Alan Taylor killed my grandfather.* Her usual passion for carefully selecting flowers evaporated, and instead she found herself ripping off petals and throwing them into the air.

Though the balance of her visit was filled with interesting activities, Kate was distracted and only wanted to get back home. No matter how hard she tried, she couldn't get Alan Taylor's name out of her mind. How dare he treat her grandpa that way! The man she adored with all her heart. "Alan Taylor," she heard herself saying again and again. "I don't know who you are or where you live, but one day I'll find you, and you'll pay for what you've done."

* * * *

With the holidays over, Kate returned back to school. The upcoming term would require diligent studying; passing the July exams was a pre-requisite for advancement to the sixth form. Kate was able to focus on her work. Her free time was a different matter. The nagging thought that had been with her since the Easter break would often return. She had a score to settle with Alan Taylor. It would have to wait, but she promised herself it was something she would never forget.

One morning, Kate was talking with her classmate and friend, Angela Pearson. Angela had been helping set up displays in the school library for the upcoming Careers Week. Those students who'd decided to leave at the end of term would have an opportunity to meet two specialists for advice on employment possibilities.

Angela was one of the students who'd decided to leave at terms end, something that had surprised Kate. "Why do you want to leave now? You're one of the brightest girls in our year, and I'm certain you'll be accepted at a top university."

"Thanks for the compliment, but I'm not interested in a professional career. I have a steady boyfriend I adore. I expect we'll be married and starting a family in a few years from now. I'm looking for an office job in the interim, and I'll probably take evening classes to learn shorthand and typing. By the way, all students can be excused from class to attend Careers Week. Why don't you come with me?"

To put an end to Angela's incessant nagging, Kate decided to skip Geography and accompany her friend. At two o'clock, they went to the library, where Angela headed straight to the area set up for administrative office jobs. To kill time, Kate browsed at the brochures on display. One caught her attention. It dealt with careers in construction management, and her thoughts went instantly to Alan Taylor, reigniting the hatred that frequently ran through her mind.

She picked up the brochure and pondered. Would pursuing construction management provide a worthwhile career? Inwardly, she knew it wasn't the job that had sparked her interest. She wrestled with her conscience for a few minutes and then she made a decision.

"Good afternoon, Mr. Pittman," she said to the gentleman who had his name printed on a tag pinned to his shirt. "My name is Kate Elliott, and I'm interested in construction management."

Mr. Pittman was perplexed. In his fifteen years of experience, he'd never had a young lady express such an interest. He thought carefully, wanting to be sensitive with his response. "Well, Miss Elliott, while there's no express exclusion, it's not a career typically pursued by females."

Keith Pittman was expecting Kate would go and look for other possibilities. To his astonishment, she seemed unfazed. "I understand, but it's still the direction I'd like to go in," she replied politely.

Following another attempt to suggest other options, Mr. Pittman advised Kate to apply to the North London College of Building that ran a two-year course in construction management. To qualify, she would have to pass five GCE "O" levels, two of which needed to be English Language and Mathematics. While Mr. Pittman was a little annoyed that Kate had disregarded his advice, he had a grudging admiration for her spirit.

CHAPTER 19

Stuart Appleton was the course director at the North London College of Building. It was summer break and his duties required him to interview potential students for the upcoming National diploma course that would begin in September. He'd received eighteen applications. Based on past experience, these would likely be filtered down to approximately fifteen suitable individuals, a number he considered ideal. Stuart had worked his way through several applications, making appropriate notes for interview dates and questions he had. On opening the next application, his first reaction was that it had been misdirected. He read it again and verified that it was indeed for the National Diploma course. He began to wonder if Kate could possibly be a boy's name. It didn't seem likely, though Stuart considered that many of the recent immigrants to England had names that made it difficult to identify their gender. Looking more carefully, his doubt was removed. The short accompanying note was signed by Miss Kate Elliott. He decided to show it to the college principal to get his take on the matter.

At first, Principal Harding was mildly amused. The notion of a female joining the next course was unthinkable. Having mulled it over, however, Harding realized they may have a problem on their hands. He was aware that county administrators had followed up on recent complaints concerning academic prejudice against females. He was hoping for a promotion to a university position, and he didn't want any potentially damaging issues on his record. "Let me sleep on it. We'll talk further tomorrow."

In the middle of dinner, James Harding's wife asked about his day. He was telling her about the administrative work, when he remembered the application Stuart Appleton had shown him.

"You'll never guess what, Doris," he said in a rather loud voice. "We received an application for the National Diploma course from a young lady."

He pulled a face at his wife and started chuckling. "I suppose now that we're in the so-called 'swinging sixties,' one has to expect all kinds of outrageous things."

He continued to laugh until he noticed that Doris hadn't joined in.

"So, what are you going to do about it?" she asked.

"I think we'll tell her she'd be wasting her time. She'll never be able to get a job in the construction industry, at least not in any managerial capacity. I'm sure she'll accept this advice and seek a more suitable course of action."

Doris looked at James sternly, "Tell me why women are denied the opportunity of managerial roles in the construction industry? Surely they should be judged on their ability, not their sex?"

James tried to think of an appropriate response. He hadn't managed to come up with one when his wife continued, "And it doesn't help the plight of women if they're denied the education necessary to get such a job."

Doris stared at her husband. Then she strutted off to the kitchen carrying the empty plates.

In the process of washing up, Doris thought about her own situation. She'd been working for a finance company for many years. Every time openings for advancement had occurred, they had always been given to men, most of whom, in her opinion, were less qualified than she was.

Doris brought dessert from the kitchen, which she and her husband ate in silence. Wishing to set a more conciliatory tone, James asked Doris if she had any suggestions.

"Even if the young lady has little chance of finding a job, don't you think she's entitled to try? It's noble of you to be candid, but I don't think it's your position to stand in the way of her aspirations."

James sensed the opportunity to take the middle ground and then move on to another subject. "Doris, I think you're correct. I'm going to tell Stuart tomorrow to do exactly what you suggested."

James smiled, hoping he'd closed the door on this topic of conversation. But Doris continued. "You may have a situation that could be used to your advantage, in addition to doing the right thing."

James looked puzzled. "Could you elaborate on that, please?"

"If you were the first construction college principal to enroll a woman, you might eventually be considered a pioneer in the world of ending gender discrimination. I'm quite sure things will change over time."

The following morning James invited Stuart Appleton to join him in his study. He adopted a studious look, "I've been thinking about that young woman's application. On reflection, I think we need to focus on education and not the prevailing habits and biases of employers. I believe things will change, and frankly it's high time they did. After all, why shouldn't women have the same opportunities as men, especially if they're equally qualified? I think it's our duty to encourage young women, and now we have an opportunity to do so."

Initially, Stuart thought James was saying all this tongue-in-cheek. When he realized James was serious he asked, "What is it you want me to do then?"

"My dear chap, we're now more than halfway through the twentieth century. Get the young lady enrolled straight away!"

With that, he showed Stuart the door and marched off to his next meeting, muttering under his breath, "Good old Doris."

* * * *

Having been accepted by the North London College of Building, Kate sought the advice of her uncle Harold, the only family member to receive an education beyond the age of fifteen.

"Being the only female in an otherwise male environment, it's highly likely you'll be subjected to the type of attention you'd prefer to do without. Try to ignore it if at all possible. Should something truly inappropriate take place, address the matter immediately. Avoid unnecessary arguments, particularly in front of others, and always behave in a calm and thoughtful manner. Also, try to show a little tolerance; you probably know by now that, typically, boys don't mature as quickly as girls. Last of all, never forget the goal. That's to get an education and pass the exams."

Kate took an early train, anxious to be prompt on her first day. Gathering in the form room, Mr. Appleton introduced the students to Mr. Stone, their class tutor. Phillip Stone requested silence, providing each student an opportunity to present themselves. When it came Kate's turn, it was obvious that many of the boys were shocked to find a female in the class.

The two-hour orientation was followed by a tour of the facilities and then a question-and-answer session. On the train ride home, Kate reflected on the day. It had been informative, though at times uncomfortable. In addition to her classmates, it was clear that many of the lecturers were also surprised at finding a young woman present.

College days passed quickly, and her uncle's advice proved to be an effective antidote to the occasional inappropriate comment. Weeks turned into months, and it soon became time to prepare for the end-of-year exams. Kate had become friendly with Andy Jennings and John Clark, so the three of them met regularly in the prep room to review the year's classwork. Kate found Andy amusing and enjoyed his company, but she was more attracted to John. Her prime focus remained on her work, reminding herself of the only reason she'd chosen to study construction management.

* * * *

Three weeks into the summer break, Kate received an unexpected phone call from John Clark, inquiring about her exam results. He seemed genuinely pleased that she'd passed, and in turn she was happy to find he had as well. Assuming the exams to be the only reason for his call, she was pleasantly surprised when he asked if she was interested in a visit to St. Paul's Cathedral. He had two complimentary tickets for a guided tour of a building they'd studied in their history class.

Kate marveled at the amazing architecture they'd learned about in their lessons. What made the day particularly special was spending time alone with John. With the tour over, they stopped at a café for tea and enjoyed a lively discussion on a variety of subjects. What had already been an exhilarating day for Kate was made even more special when John escorted her to the train station and warmly kissed her on the cheek.

* * * *

With the new term approaching, Lilly took Kate clothes shopping. "I've always thought that one feels better about themselves if they're nicely dressed," Lilly told her grand-daughter. "Your grandpa was the same way. Without wasting money, he believed I should always look my best."

Kate had long admired her grandma's taste, which had clearly rubbed off on her mother. Shopping with Grandma Lilly was always a joy. She never rushed, and she allowed Kate to try on all the outfits that took her fancy. She only offered advice if she was asked, but Kate always sought her input, knowing she'd never be disappointed.

She was thrilled with her new outfits, which she thought very fetching, indeed. She wondered if John would notice. Clothes didn't appear to figure high on his priorities; he invariably wore old jeans and baggy sweaters.

With the second year underway, classwork and home-work ramped up significantly. Kate knuckled down. She didn't want to risk failing her finals.

Several students had mentioned the upcoming Christmas dance that would be held at the adjacent College of Arts and Crafts. Kate hadn't made up her mind whether to attend or not. When Andy and John confirmed that they were going, it made her decision easy.

It turned out to be a wonderful event, and Kate spent the entire evening on the dance floor; jiving to the Rolling Stones and the Beatles, twisting to the new sound from America, Chubby Checker, and finally, join-ing in a long chain, chugging around the hall to Little Eva's "Locomotion." Delighting in the excitement all around her, Kate was disappointed when the disc jockey announced the final number. She, of course, was unaware that the most memorable part of the evening was still to unfold. It took place at the train station, where, for the first time, John kissed her passionately.

The new term flew by, and in what seemed like the blink of an eye, finals were approaching. At this point in the year, the class tutor offered his students consultation on future employment, a subject that had been on Kate's mind for some while.

Kate's appointment with Mr. Stone turned out to be somewhat of a disappointment. Though he clearly had good intentions, it became evident that his practical knowledge of the industry was limited and outdated. While he'd heard of Taylor Construction, he knew little about their business or who they might be associated with. He was able to provide the names of two companies who'd employed students in the past and a template that could be used when applying for a job.

Following her meeting with Mr. Stone, Kate asked John if they could talk in private. They'd never discussed employment, and she was keen to know if he had any plans or ideas that he might share.

"Fortunately, I've had something lined up for a long time. Of course, it's subject to my passing finals," John said.

"Really, how were you able to do that, if you don't mind my asking?"

"It's a long story."

"One I'd love to hear."

"My granddad was a carpenter. He meant a lot to me, and I wanted to follow suit. I'd intended to take up an apprenticeship. Granddad said I would do better going into management. Before his retirement, he worked for a local company, and was able to arrange for me to meet their personnel manager. He recommended that I obtain a National Diploma. That would be a requirement if I wanted to be considered for a management trainee position."

"I get it. That's why you enrolled for this course!"

"Exactly, when I got accepted here, I went back for a formal interview and they offered me a job subject to passing my exams."

"That's exciting, John. By the way, what's the name of the company?"

"It's Taylor Construction."

Kate's stomach tightened and she swallowed hard, "I've heard the name, but I don't know much about them."

"Apparently they've been very successful, so I'm hoping there'll be good opportunities for me. What are your plans, Kate?"

"Mr. Stone gave me the names of two firms who'd employed past students. I'll be applying to them. It might make sense to try a couple of others, and I was wondering if you had any suggestions."

John scratched his head. "To be perfectly honest, I don't know much about the industry. My granddad told me about a magazine that advertises jobs. I could get the name of it if you like."

"That would be helpful; thank you."

"I suppose I could also give you the contact information for Taylor Construction's personnel manager. Maybe they want more trainees."

Kate felt a sudden rush of excitement. "How would you feel about us being co-workers if such a possibility existed?"

"I think it could be a lot of fun. I'll bring the details with me tomorrow."

Kate reflected on her conversation with John all the way home. Disclosure of his likely future employer had shaken her. Fortunately, he hadn't appeared to notice. She mulled over the pros and cons of working for Taylor Construction versus having a friend who worked there. She decided the matter wasn't within her control, and either scenario would likely be a step toward her secret goal.

Two weeks of finals was a blur. Immediately one subject finished, Kate was engrossed in her books again preparing for the next one. The second Friday quickly arrived, and then it was all over. With the intensity of the preceding fortnight behind them, the class planned their last week together. They were looking forward to letting off steam and then enjoying their last summer break.

All students were required to attend college for the remaining week of term. Having checked in with their form tutor, they were allowed to do whatever they wished. Kate's class took advantage of the two members who owned cars. Every day, they would pile in and tour the neighborhood, taking photographs of each other in comical poses, and visiting a trendy coffee bar where they listened to the latest pop music. Kate reveled in the camaraderie, and though she rarely participated in the outrageous comments and gestures her fellow students made, she laughed heartily at their antics.

On the final day, Kate exchanged phone numbers with several classmates, and they promised to stay in touch. Every last boy gave her a hug, wishing her the best, and some kissed her cheek. With the goodbyes over, John walked Kate to the train station. They stopped at the entrance for a final embrace.

"What are your plans for the summer holidays? I'd like to see you if possible. I'm also keen to find out about the responses you get from your job applications." John said.

"I might have the odd weekend away visiting family. I'll be home most of the time. You're more than welcome to visit whenever you like. I think you know by now that I always enjoy your company."

John took hold of Kate's hands, "If it were left up to me, I'd be there almost every day. You're starting to grow on me kiddo. Having spent the last two years seeing you nearly every day," he said, taking her in his arms.

"Give me a call, and we can make arrangements" Kate said, indulging herself in one final kiss.

Running down the stairs to the train platform, Kate had an extra bounce in her step. With college days behind her, she could enjoy the six-week break, especially knowing that she would be able to continue seeing John. She was confident of passing her exams. The next big step was getting a job. On the journey home, Kate's mind turned to Alan Taylor. More than two years had passed since she'd first heard his name. Her resolve to get even with him had not diminished one iota.

* * * *

Arriving back home from a weekend visit with her aunt and uncle, Kate found three letters waiting for her.

"Perhaps you should open them in private," Kate's mother said, seeing her daughter's reaction to the senders' names.

"Whatever news they bring, I'd like to share with you and Grandma," Kate replied, ripping open the first one from Riley Brothers.

Rita and Lilly looked on anxiously while Kate read the letter. They didn't need to guess its content when she started jumping for joy. A great start, Kate thought to herself; things were only going to get better. She also had an interview with Winter Construction, and the third envelope confirmed she had successfully passed her National Diploma exam.

Unable to contain herself, she phoned John. "I've got two interviews!" she said gleefully. "One is with Riley Brothers, and another one with Winter Construction." She hesitated, adding delicately, "I also passed my exams." She prayed that John had, too.

"Congratulations. And yes, somehow I must have fooled those people up in Cambridge, because I passed as well."

To her relief, Kate said, "That's great news, John, I'm so happy for you. I assume that confirms your employment. Do you have a starting date?"

"My first day is the 31st of August. Which reminds me, did you hear back from Taylor Construction?"

"No, I didn't. And given the amount of time that's passed, I don't expect to," Kate said, unable to disguise her disappointment.

"I assume they didn't have any openings. The least they could have done was to write and let you know,"

John said, feeling a tinge of guilt at having provided Kate with the contact.

"I suppose so," Kate said gently, realizing that she may have appeared ungrateful for John's introduction.

"Would you like to get together sometime soon?" John asked, thinking it best to change the subject."

"I'd love to, would this weekend work for you?"

"It certainly will."

On Saturday, the young couple went for a walk through the park and for lunch they enjoyed fish and chips.

"You've got a big week ahead, Kate. Back to back interviews. I'm betting that in a couple of weeks from now, you'll have the option of working for whichever company you like best."

"I wish I could share your optimism. I'm not sure why, but I feel a little nervous."

"No reason to. Your high grades speak for themselves. I'm sure both firms would be happy to recruit someone with your talent."

That evening, John took Kate to the early performance at the cinema, a treat to celebrate their exam results. Kate felt very romantic, holding hands with John throughout the film. At its conclusion, his imminent departure made her a little sad. "I've had a wonderful day; I wish you didn't have to leave," she said, giving him a final hug at the train station.

"I feel the same way, Kate. Next week, I'll be busy visiting family. I can see you the following week if that works. By then, I'm sure you will have a job so we can celebrate again." John said, giving Kate a last passionate kiss that sent shivers racing through her body.

* * * *

Once again, Grandma Lilly had promised to buy Kate new outfits, this time for her upcoming interviews. On Monday morning, they set off to the West End and spent a joyful day flitting around numerous shops. Kate finally settled on a two-piece, navy-blue skirt and jacket combination, together with a grey trouser suit. Afterward, they went for an early dinner. "You look stunning in your new outfits, my dear," Lilly told her granddaughter.

"Thanks, Grandma. I'm looking forward to the interviews, though I must say I'm a nervous wreck."

"Just relax, and be yourself. Anyone with half a brain can tell you're a smart young lady."

On Wednesday morning, Kate boarded the train for her 10:30 a.m. interview with Riley Brothers. She checked in with the receptionist who escorted her to Mr. Gibbon's office. "What made you interested in the construction industry?" was his opening question.

Kate told him about her family history in the business, saying she wanted to continue this tradition. She was hoping to get some favorable reaction, but Mr. Gibbons remained poker-faced. Instead of asking more about her desires, he boorishly ran over several routine matters that Kate thought she'd already addressed in her application. With little enthusiasm, he glanced at his watch and then asked, "Do you have any questions for me?"

Kate's tutor had told her to be prepared for this. "I'd appreciate receiving more details on the company training program."

Mr. Gibbons pulled a booklet from his desk drawer and handed it over. Kate was about to ask a follow-up question when Mr. Gibbons said, "Thank you for visiting today, Miss Elliott. You'll be hearing from us shortly."

On her way home, Kate relived her brief meeting. She had nothing to compare it with but couldn't help feeling that it hadn't gone well. She told her mother and grandmother about it later. "It was obvious he had no interest in me from the moment I arrived. I've no doubt that he was asking himself why a woman wanted to be in the construction industry."

"Perhaps he didn't need to ask you much. After all, you passed your exams," Lilly said, trying to be supportive when she sensed her granddaughter's disappointment.

* * * *

Two days later, Kate set off for her interview with Winter Construction. She'd expected to meet Mr. Grimes, but on arrival, she was informed that he was out sick, and Mr. Henderson would be taking his place. A few minutes later, a tall individual with thick, horn-rimmed glasses appeared. "Good morning, Miss Elliott," he said, leading Kate to his office.

Once seated, Mr. Henderson opened a white binder, and in the process of reading the contents he appeared confused. "Can you please confirm that you've applied for a position as a management trainee?" he asked.

Although his question caught Kate off guard, she remained composed. "That's correct," she said firmly.

Mr. Henderson started to fidget. "Would you by chance have any interest in an administrative position?"

"No sir, I've just passed the National Diploma exams, and I'm looking for something in the management field."

"We've had more than one woman who started out in our typing pool and ended up becoming an executive secretary," Mr. Henderson said hopefully. The look of disgust that appeared on Kate's face didn't require explanation. Perceiving the predicament he found himself in, Mr. Henderson said, "Let me discuss this matter further with some of my colleagues. I'll write to you in a week or so to let you know what we might be able to offer."

Kate was boiling with frustration. Once outside the front entrance, she shouted aloud, "Why bother getting an education! You stupid, ignorant, old-fashioned bugger!" Her outburst startled several people passing by. At the same moment, Mr. Henderson was wondering why on earth Mr. Grimes had arranged to interview a young woman for a position he knew senior management would never agree to.

By the time Kate arrived home, she'd cooled down a little. Over dinner, she told her mother and grandmother the details of her interview.

"It sounds so unfair," Lilly said, "but you must never give up. Both your mother and I know you have the ability, and I'm sure you'll get another opportunity soon. I know you weren't optimistic about the other interview. You may still be pleasantly surprised."

Kate decided to wait for the news from Riley Brothers before doing anything further. On Saturday she telephoned John.

"How did the interviews go?" he asked eagerly.

"Not very well, I'm afraid. I doubt I'll be getting an offer from either firm."

"I think you're just being pessimistic. I'm betting that when we meet up next Saturday you'll have a job!"

On Wednesday, a letter from Riley Brothers arrived. It said they'd filled their requirements for management trainees, adding that Kate could apply again next year if she wished. The following day, another letter arrived from Winter Construction. It offered a position for a junior typist. Normally even tempered, Kate took the letter into the garden where she set it alight, taking great pleasure in stamping on the resulting ashes. Understanding the need to regroup and start another search, she decided to discuss it with John on his next visit.

At the weekend, Kate took John to her local park where they sat on a bench to chat. "You would have lost your bet," Kate said gruffly.

"Sorry, I'm not sure what you mean."

"I got turned down by both companies. Well, technically, I suppose I did get an offer to join the typing pool. That was only adding insult to injury."

Kate's news astounded John. He knew she was a better all-around student than him. "To be honest, I feel a little embarrassed. How could I have a job while you don't? It doesn't make sense. The last two years have demonstrated you're a notch above me."

Kate smiled. "That's very kind of you even if it's not true. Never mind, I'm sure something will crop up," she said, putting on a brave face.

John promised to visit again in two weeks and encouraged Kate to start job hunting straight away.

CHAPTER 20

John Clark had been working at Taylor Construction for six weeks. He was pleased with his progress, but his concern for Kate had steadily increased. It hadn't taken him long to find out the industry was dominated by males, and that Kate almost certainly wasn't getting a fair shot.

One morning, John's manager told him there was a short-term crunch in the estimating group. There'd been an uptick in potential new projects, necessitating additional help for a few weeks in order to cope. John welcomed the opportunity; he believed it would broaden his knowledge. The following day, he was introduced to the senior estimator, Peter Walker.

"Good morning, John, I'm pleased to have you on board. I know you're new to the industry. Having successfully completed the National Diploma course, I assume you're comfortable measuring material quantities?"

"I think so. Hopefully, I can get some help if need be. I'd hate to mess up and cause a problem."

"Don't worry about that. Signing off on your work is my responsibility. If you have any questions, just give me a shout. All I ask is that you clearly label your assumptions. That will make it easier for me to check."

* * * *

John had been working under Peter's direction for one month when he overheard him telling his boss, Dick Casey, he'd like the assistance to continue for a few more weeks. Dick told him he'd promised the project manager that John would only be needed for a maximum of five weeks, so he'd have to come up with an alternate plan.

Toward the end of the day, a thought flashed through John's mind. "Excuse me, Peter. I couldn't help overhearing your conversation with Mr. Casey earlier. I have a friend who was in my class at college. She's very talented, and she's looking for a job."

"You said 'she.' I assume you're referring to a female?"

John felt his face burning. He'd pegged Peter to be an open-minded person. Now, he wasn't sure. "Yes, I am," he said hesitantly.

Peter looked thoughtful. Then a broad smile crossed his face. "You know, John, I think that could be very interesting. Between you and me, I've often wondered why we've never engaged a female in this department. I know it's hard to find suitable candidates. I suppose the reluctance to hire women just creates a vicious cycle. It's obvious why females choose not to study construction—its damn near impossible for them to get a job." Peter said. "I'll have to ask Dick for his permission. Personally, I like the idea."

When the work day was over, John told Kate about his conversation with Peter. While she was grateful for his thoughtfulness, she doubted that anything would come of it. The next evening her phone rang. "Guess what! Your temporary employment has been approved. You start work at nine o'clock next Monday." John shouted down the line.

"Oh, I'm so grateful!" Kate called out when she got her breath back. "Could we meet up this weekend? I'd like to get some insight on the type of work I'll be doing."

Kate was not looking forward to telling her mother and grandma about the short-term appointment. To her relief, they offered their congratulations without further comment: though she was sure her grandma twitched at the mention of Taylor Construction.

Peter Walker was waiting in the reception hall on Monday morning. "Good morning, Kate. Welcome to Taylor Construction. Let me show you where you'll be working and give you a quick tour of the office. Then we can get down to business. We've got a lot on our plate, so I'm pleased you're here to help."

"Thank you, Mr. Walker. I'm very grateful for the opportunity."

He smiled, and led Kate to the estimating department. It was spacious and well lit, furnished with stainless steel chairs and laminate-topped tables. "This will be your desk," Peter said, taking Kate on a whirlwind tour of the major departments. Back at Kate's workspace, Peter gave her a set of drawings, explaining which materials he wanted her to measure. "Let me know when you've finished, and we can review your work together. I'll be doing some double checking, so don't get overly concerned about making a mistake. I know this may be more challenging than the work you were given at college. I'm confident you'll soon get the hang of it." Peter pulled a face in fun. "Especially given the outstanding recommendation I received from your college buddy."

"I suspect John may have complimented me beyond that which I deserve," Kate responded, looking a trifle embarrassed.

"And I suspect you're being overly modest, young lady! Let's see how it goes."

Office hours were nine to five-thirty, and at day's end, Kate was still engrossed in her work.

"Time for you to call it a day," Peter exclaimed.

"I'm nearly finished," Kate replied. "Maybe another thirty minutes."

"It will keep till morning. Have a pleasant evening, and we'll review your work tomorrow."

Kate tidied her desk and took off to meet John at a local pub. They'd arranged to go separately; being seen leaving together may give the wrong impression. Charging through the entrance door with her face beaming, Kate ran toward John, threw her arms around him, and kissed him on the lips, "My hero," she said. "I'm so indebted to you."

The next morning, Kate met with Peter to review her first assignment. He ran over her work in detail, noting her neat and methodical approach. Random checks on her math confirmed consistent accuracy. "Well done, Kate.

I can tell you'll fit in here, and I really need someone I can rely on."

With each subsequent assignment, Peter became more impressed with Kate's ability. The workload wasn't letting up, so at the conclusion of her four-week engagement, Peter asked Dick Casey if he could extend the arrangement. "If she's that good, go ahead," Dick said.

Sensing an opportunity, Peter decided to take it a step further. "Actually, I'd like to recommend that she become a permanent junior estimator. I've always relied on support from trainees. Whilst I appreciate the help, I often spend more time checking and correcting their work than I would by doing it myself. In Kate Elliott's case, it's totally different. She picks things up quickly, works hard, and rarely makes a mistake. Another great characteristic is that she doesn't hesitate to ask questions. Something I find refreshing."

"You may have a point. I'd like to meet with her before making that decision."

Dick Casey had only ever seen Kate from a distance, and she'd always had her head down working. Now, standing tall in a navy blue suit and high heels, he saw how attractive she was. He'd never dealt with a female estimator, and in talking to Kate, he found his eyes wandering. Despite finding this uncomfortable, she didn't allow herself to be distracted or lose focus. "I think you'll be an excellent addition to our department. We'd like to offer you a permanent position with a starting salary of nine pounds a week," Dick concluded with a smile, thinking he would like to get to know Kate better in the future.

"Thank you Mr. Casey, I really appreciate that. I assure you I'll do my best at all times."

"I know you will, Kate. Perhaps we'll have lunch together after you've settled in."

Kate was ecstatic. Not only did it fulfill her growing need for a regular income, it would also help her hidden agenda. She hadn't appreciated Dick Casey's roving eye and flirtatious manner. Still, he was a senior member of staff and perhaps his ways may eventually prove to be advantageous. There was much for her to think about and digest. While she was anxious to move forward, she knew it was wise to take one small step at a time.

* * * *

News of Kate's hiring spread like wildfire, resulting in much comment and speculation; none more so than at the end table in the canteen where female members from the typing pool and accounts department ate lunch each day. "I'm encouraged," Pauline said. "About time a woman in this company is recognized for her brains."

"Has anyone spoken to her, because she looks snooty to me?" Ada asked.

"I think you're just jealous," Deirdre retorted. "Nothing wrong with a female wanting to get ahead, and I expect she needs to act the part."

"Depends how she got the job," Jill chimed in.

"What do you mean by that?" Shirley asked.

Haughtily, Jill shot back. "I mean it may have been a result of who she slept with."

"Given the department she works in, it could well have been Dick Casey. I've heard he's a randy old sod," Sally added.

"Well, you should know," Jill replied, pulling a face at Sally.

"He only gave me a lift home," Sally said, blushing profusely.

"Next you'll be telling us his car wouldn't start until you took your bra off," Jill jabbed back, a remark that caused the entire table to fall about in hysterical laughter.

* * * *

Now a permanent staff member, Kate met Peter Walker each Monday morning to run over her previous week's work. Gradually the role expanded to include trade bid comparisons, which helped broaden her knowledge of contract terms and conditions. In the process of analyzing four plumbing bids, an idea sprang to mind. That evening, Kate mentioned her current assignment to her grandma.

"Did grandpa do his own estimating, or did he employ someone to help him?"

"He had an estimator for many years," Lilly replied, a serene look spreading across her face as she cast her mind back. "He was a real gentleman, and George thought the world of him."

Casually, Kate asked, "Did I ever meet him?"

"I'm not sure, my dear. He came to the house on several occasions. I don't remember if you were home at the time."

"I suppose he's retired by now?" Kate said cautiously. She didn't want her grandma to become suspicious of the real motive behind her question.

"No, Arthur's still relatively young. Interestingly enough, I bumped into him recently. He now works for a firm in Harlow."

It had taken a considerable amount of phone calls, but three days later, Kate discovered a Mr. Arthur Thomas was the chief estimator at Downey Mechanical and Plumbing contractors based in Harlow.

* * * *

Caught up in the excitement of having tracked down an individual who may be able to help with her quest, Kate realized she'd overlooked asking Arthur for a way of identifying him. Hoping for inspiration while scanning the patrons seated in the Chinese restaurant, she felt a light tap on the shoulder. "Hello, Kate," said a man with fair hair and pale green eyes. "I'm Arthur Thomas, and oh my, how you've grown up."

"Hello, Mr. Thomas. I assume we've met. I have to admit I don't remember."

"Not in person, to the best of my recollection. I recognized you from the photograph your grandfather kept in his office. I've reserved a table. Let's get seated, and I'll see if I can answer your questions."

With their orders placed, Kate decided to come clean quickly. "Mr. Thomas," she started out, feeling her cheeks blushing.

"Please, call me Arthur," her host interjected.

Kate cleared her throat. "Arthur, I wasn't totally forthright with you on the phone. When I've explained the background, I sincerely hope you'll understand and forgive me."

Arthur frowned, "I'm intrigued," he said.

"A few years ago, I inadvertently discovered more about my grandpa's demise than my grandma would have wished. I was very close to my grandfather. When I heard what had taken place, I promised myself I'd seek justice if at all possible."

Arthur was taken back. "I assume you're referring to the Crescent Street Project?" he asked tentatively. He wanted to make sure they weren't talking at cross purposes.

"That's correct," Kate replied. "Yes, the project where Alan Taylor cheated my grandpa."

Kate's passion was clear for Arthur to see. Her eyes were glazed. "Does your grandma know you are aware of this?"

"No, and I hope to keep it that way. I'm certain she would like to see those responsible punished. At the same time, I know she'd be worried sick if she thought I was getting involved with dastardly characters."

"I understand," Arthur said, contemplating the matter for a moment or two. "Rest assured she won't hear a word from me."

"Thank you, Arthur. Now let me get my next untruth out of the way. I'm not looking for a job with a plumbing company. I'm already employed by Taylor Construction."

Arthur was unable to hide his amazement. He said louder than intended, "Goodness gracious! I'm going to choke on my sweet and sour if you spring any more surprises like that."

"I'm very sorry about the deceptions. I thought if I told you my real motives, you'd refuse to meet me."

Arthur rested his elbows on the table and reflected. "Kate, I think you're a very brave girl, but you need to be careful. I wouldn't underestimate Alan Taylor if I were you. I think he'd go to any lengths to get what he wants." Arthur thought he noticed Kate shudder. "Like you, I thought the world of your grandfather. He gave me my first real start and mentored me for many years. I'd be willing to help in any way I can. Again, I caution you to be very careful."

"I appreciate your concern and I'm grateful. At this point I'm just trying to find out all I can about what happened. I think that will help me figure out my next steps."

For the remainder of lunch, Arthur recapped the history of events leading up to the award of the Crescent Street Project. "Clearly Alan Taylor was the mastermind. At first, we assumed Frank Ward was in on it, though, like Dick Casey, he was probably just carrying out instructions, unaware of the overall plot. There's no doubt the form was switched. Though Alan's secretary played a role, I'm certain she had no idea what was happening either."

"I know there was an investigation. Were you involved in that?" Kate asked; she couldn't remember the details of what she'd heard while sitting in her aunt's passageway.

"Your grandma and I had a meeting with the police and the company solicitor. I told them what I thought had happened. They launched a preliminary enquiry. Eventually they determined there wasn't enough evidence to persuade the prosecutor to take action. Your grandma decided to drop the matter. She didn't want it discussed further, thinking it would be better for George's memory if his death was just left an unfortunate accident."

"I really appreciate the information, Arthur. Thanks again for your support. I've already met Dick Casey, and I believe I have access to him if need be. That could be useful. My gut tells me that I've got to get closer to Alan or Frank. That could prove to be very difficult," Kate said.

*   *   *   *

Kate had been working at the company for three months. She had assumed securing her job would automatically provide an opportunity to set eyes on Alan Taylor for the first time. She began to wonder if he intentionally stayed away from the production areas. Now that she'd grown a little closer to Peter Walker, she felt comfortable asking him about this.

"Very few people get to meet Alan Taylor," Peter explained. "His office is in the penthouse suite; only executives have access. Oh, with one exception," he added as an afterthought.

"Who might that be?" Kate asked tentatively, hoping she wasn't overstepping the mark.

"Miss Penny Trent. I've heard several theories about her relationship with Alan Taylor and Frank Ward. Of course, most are likely nothing more than gossip. All I know for sure is that at one time she managed the canteen. Apparently, she was later promoted, working directly for Frank and Alan. She may have had past ties to them. I really don't know."

"What does she do now?"

"I'm not sure of the particulars. All I've heard is that she arranges entertainment for potential clients. It's anyone's guess what that might entail."

Kate's first sight of Alan Taylor was an unplanned event. Peter Walker was taking her to an internal meeting when Alan suddenly appeared in the corridor. Peter made a brief introduction, and immediately Kate felt herself shaking. He was taller than she'd expected. Despite a masculine look, with his slicked back dark hair, long sideburns, and piercing brown eyes, he gave her the creeps. He only stopped briefly to say hello. That was sufficient time for Kate to feel the hatred rushing through her veins. *Now I know who you are and what you look like. Beware—I'll find a way to get even with you, you pig,* Kate heard herself think.

A week after setting eyes on Alan Taylor for the first time, Kate received a call from Dick Casey, inviting her to lunch. Now aware of his involvement in the Crescent Street Project, she was keen to develop a relationship, thinking it may help provide further information.

Knowing that Peter would be better informed on Dick's interests, she sought his advice.

"Just remain professional and let Dick take the lead. I expect he'll do that, anyway."

Peter's vague response surprised Kate. It wasn't typical of his straightforward manner. She wondered if he was holding something back, or trying to tip her off. She toyed with the idea of seeking clarification, but decided that wasn't tactful, at least not yet.

Dick took Kate to a nearby restaurant where they discussed her current assignment. Kate thought the meeting was going very well, until Dick asked if she had a boyfriend and added an inappropriate innuendo. Kate was a little flustered. She hoped it was just a one-off comment. It soon became clear that it wasn't. Throughout lunch, Dick was unrelenting, becoming more and more personal and flirtatious.

On her return to the office, Peter enquired about her meeting. Kate faltered; unconvincingly, she said, "All things considered, I thought it went quite well."

Peter picked up on the underlying message. "Dick is my boss. He's next in line to be the chief estimator. He's competent, but, well, I'd suggest you keep your distance, if you know what I mean."

Instead of responding, Kate simply gave Peter a knowing look, confident the unspoken word had been received and understood.

CHAPTER 21

"You must visit this weekend," John told Kate excitedly. He and Andy Jennings had placed a rental deposit on a two-bedroom apartment.

"I'd love to. I've a feeling you only want me to show you where the kitchen is and how the appliances work," Kate said teasingly. John had long since acknowledged his lack of acumen in domestic matters.

"You're probably right. Andy tells me he's a good cook, and I know where the launderette is," John said playfully.

"Just as well, otherwise you'd soon be running around in only your underwear," Kate replied, prolonging the jovial banter she and John had come to enjoy.

Since joining Taylor Construction, seven months' prior, Kate's friendship with John had continued to blossom. Her grandma gave her one of George's old company cars for her nineteenth birthday, which enabled her to take John on excursions at weekends. For professional reasons they continued to keep their relationship away from co-workers. They were acutely aware of their growing attachment, a subject John raised at a weekend picnic. "You know Kate you're the only girl I have eyes for. But I'm glad we're establishing our careers before taking things further."

Kate was content with John's assessment. It both matched her feelings and reflected his maturity. Additionally, it gave her time to accomplish another goal.

* * * *

In her early weeks at the company, Kate ate lunch at her desk. When she'd settled in she started visiting the staff canteen and this enabled her to meet co-workers. Initially, some of them had been wary. Over time Kate broke the ice. Having done so, she was invited to join the group of women who always assembled at the end table. Each day a range of topics were discussed, which invariably included the latest office gossip. One lunch time, Kate arrived to find Joan Green eating on her own. "Where is everyone?" Kate asked.

"There's a sale at the clothing store in Brent Street," Joan replied.

"Why didn't you go?"

"I think their fashions are for girls a little younger than me," Joan said in a self- deprecating tone.

Kate guessed Joan to be in her late forties, and finding her alone provided an opportunity to discuss more personal matters. Upon discovering Joan was divorced, Kate asked if she was dating.

"Not really, but there's a chap I see occasionally."

"Do you think it will develop into something more permanent?" Kate asked tactfully.

"I don't think his wife would be too keen on that," Joan replied.

Kate smiled. Though she didn't approve of such behavior, it provided an appropriate opportunity to ask about the latest goings on. Joan glanced around to make sure she couldn't be overheard. "There's nearly always something titillating happening in this place."

She proceeded to inform Kate that Jenny in accounts was having an affair with her manager. If Kate wanted to get the full scoop she should talk to Sally Banks.

"Is that the same Sally who normally sits at this table?" Kate asked.

"Yes, it's hard to miss her. She always wears a skirt that looks more like a wide belt," Joan said, laughing at her own joke.

"Now I know who you mean," said Kate, smiling. "I suppose if you've got it, why not flaunt it?"

Joan smirked. "You're right, she does have shapely legs. At a guess I'd say half the young men in this company have checked them out from top to bottom."

The two women laughed out loud. "I assume you are just kidding," Kate said when they settled back down.

Joan took on a more serious look, "Sally is a nice young girl, but she's naïve and man crazy. Trust me when I tell you, those characteristics come to the forefront when she's been drinking. I've no doubt that many of her alleged indulgencies have been exaggerated, but she told me about one of her amazing escapades."

Kate's curiosity was aroused, "Really?"

"This is just between you and me. I happened to go to the pub a few weeks ago and ended up talking with Sally. At first we had a meaningful conversation. Three drinks later her speech got louder and faster, and then she started using off-color language and telling very personal stories. I've met girls with similar traits. Without a doubt, Sally leads the pack. When she's completely bombed, her tongue gets looser and looser, and, I suspect, that also applies to the elastic in her panties. She went on to tell me she'd had sex with Alan Taylor."

Joan placed her forefinger on her lips and pulled a face. "I suppose your job security improves if you've been in the sack with the big boss."

* * * *

Kate knew it was unlikely she'd find Sally alone in the office. At five-twenty-five, she tidied her desk and went directly to the main entrance, knowing the typing pool workers left promptly at five-thirty. Minutes later, Sally appeared wearing a green mini skirt and a tight white sweater, an outfit that accentuated her shapely figure.

"Excuse me, Sally. We've never really had the chance to get to know each other. Perhaps we could go out for a drink one evening?"

The idea of going for a drink at any time appealed to Sally. She was also keen to find out more about the young woman who many of the company's female staff had discussed. "I always say there's no time like the present. Why don't we go now?"

Kate's grandmother was used to her working late, and dinner was always left ready to be served whatever time she arrived. Not wanting to miss the opportunity at hand, Kate drove Sally to a local pub, promising to give her a ride home afterward.

Arriving at the Bunch of Grapes, Kate went to the bar while Sally found a table.

"How long have you worked for the company?" Kate asked, handing over a double vodka tonic and sipping on the lemonade she'd purchased for herself.

"Nearly three years."

"Do you like your job?"

"Most of the time I do. I get a little bored if things are slow, but that doesn't happen very often. I'm also friendly with most of the girls, and that helps."

Kate continued to ask Sally questions about her pastimes while keeping a careful eye on her drink. With little more than ice cubes remaining in the glass, Kate asked, "Is it the same again?" heading in the direction of the bar without waiting for a reply.

Sally steadily worked her way through another drink, and in the process she began to speak a little louder, the cue Kate had been waiting for. "I think there are some very attractive men in our company, don't you?" she asked. Before Sally had the chance to respond, Kate added, "Sorry, I didn't realize your drink was that low. Let me get you another one and then we can continue our discussion."

Sally thanked Kate for her third drink, and said, "I've been out with several project managers and a bloke from the scheduling department. I've also had drinks with a few others. I'm sure it's made a number of the girls in the office jealous."

"Did you tell them who you went out with, then?" Kate whispered.

"I only mentioned the good-looking ones. If some of the girls knew who'd taken me out earlier this year, they'd be green with envy."

"And-------?" Kate said expectantly.

Sally prolonged the moment, thinking it would add significance to what she was about to reveal. "I went out with our chairman, Mr. Taylor," she said triumphantly.

"Wow. How on earth did you manage to get a date with him?"

"It's a long story. Do you happen to know Penny Trent?" Sally asked.

"I only know her by name. I've seen her on occasion. We've never actually met," Kate said, curious as to how Miss Trent fitted into the story.

"Several months ago she invited me out for a drink." Sally's face glowed with pride. "She told me Mr. Taylor thought I was attractive and that he wanted me to escort him to an important event at the Hilton Hotel. She went on to say that I needed to be appropriately outfitted and that she'd take me shopping at the weekend." Sally intentionally paused, enjoying spinning her story out. "That Saturday, I went to Miss Trent's flat and from there she took me to the West End. She purchased an evening gown, high heels, and a necklace so I would look the part. She even paid for me to have my hair done," she concluded smugly.

"How was the evening?"

"Top quality all of the way; you know—champagne, fancy food—really posh stuff." Sally's face was now glowing from both the effect of the alcohol and her past accomplishment.

"Did Mr. Taylor take you home afterward?" Kate asked, hoping Sally might offer up more details.

"He ordered a taxi for me the following morning," Sally said, sure that Kate would interpret the implication.

"Oh, you stayed up all night together?" Said Kate wide eyed.

Sally put her hands on her hips and stared in amazement. "Don't be so naïve, Kate. I spent the night making love with Alan Taylor in his penthouse suite," she said in a voice that could be heard several tables away.

"Well you're a very lucky girl," Kate whispered, conscious that the people sitting at the next table were listening, and at the same time thinking how accurate Joan Green's assessment of Sally had been.

"It's been a pleasure getting to know you," Kate told Sally, who was looking increasingly pleased with herself. "We'll have to do it again. Drink up and I'll give you a ride home."

On the journey to Sally's house, a thought crossed Kate's mind. It seemed like a long shot, but worth a try. "By the way, do you happen to remember Miss Trent's address?"

"34 Hatton Gardens," was the immediate and unexpected reply.

CHAPTER 22

Penny Trent entered the manager's office at the Sunlight Club. "I understand you wanted to see me," she said.

Ted Phillips let out a long sigh. "Take a seat, love. Would you care for a drink?" he asked unnecessarily. Penny could see he'd already poured two large glasses of gin.

"Cheers, Penny," he said, passing one to her and raising the other in the air.

Penny reciprocated. "What's the occasion?"

Ted Phillips adopted a more serious look and he reached for his pipe. "Look, Penny…" He stopped mid-sentence and took a long drag. With smoke streaming from his nostrils, he added. "You've given us great service all these years, but, well, in your game there's a natural shelf life." He paused, waiting for a reaction.

Penny reflected on the manager's words. "What are you saying, Mr. Phillips?"

"Simply put, my dear, the punters only come here because of the young ladies."

Penny's jaw slowly dropped. The manager's message registered with her. Subconsciously, she'd always known this day would come. Now it seemed so sudden, and it caught her off guard. She fidgeted, trying to come to terms with what was happening to her. She'd never wanted to be in this line of work, good grief, she could hardly think of anything worse; but it was all she had and all she knew. Her mind turned somersaults, and she felt confused. Maybe it was for the best, she tried to tell herself again and again. Being shown the door just because of her age made her feel helpless and unwanted.

Ted Phillips had been in similar situations. He didn't allow himself to become emotionally involved with the girls. "Don't take it personally. We all have to call it a day some time or other. It's just that in your profession it happens earlier than most others. In any event I'm not asking you to leave this minute. Pick your own time. I expect you may want to tell the other girls you're moving on to something better." He paused. "But I can't keep you on the payroll for more than another two weeks."

* * * *

Three days had passed since Penny's emotional rollercoaster with Ted Phillips, and during this time, she hadn't stepped outside her flat. Her mind had recounted over and over the events since her last days in the orphanage, and somehow it all seemed like a dream. She thought about the good and bad, clearly remembering the first time she'd stripped in front of a live audience.

Twenty-four years later, it still made her tremble. But that wasn't the worst of it—that was still to come. She thought back to the fateful day when Mr. Fisher sent her a note asking to see her in his office. At first, she was excited to find she'd been hand selected to entertain an important client—her excitement ended quickly when she was handed a pack of condoms. Realizing what Mr. Fisher meant by entertaining, she recalled telling him, "There's no way on God's earth I'm going to do that." More vividly, she was able to recapture the smarmy look on his face when he told her it wasn't optional if she wanted to keep her job. In her naivety, she hadn't realized that Mr. Fisher pulled 'this number' on all the girls he knew to be desperate for an income and had no other practical options. What a bastard the man really was. Over the years, her feelings toward him had softened somewhat, Lord only knows why.

And then there was Daisy, probably the only true joy in her adult life. Dear, dear Daisy. What a well-meaning sweet girl she was. Regrettably, the cards of life had dealt her a bad hand—one she couldn't handle. Penny knew that Daisy had sacrificed everything for her son, Alan. In the process, she'd lost her dignity and self-worth, and the only way she could cope was through alcohol and pills. What a bloody shame, Penny thought. She was sure that Daisy would most likely have had a wonderful life if not for an unfortunate chance meeting with Derek Taylor.

Penny knew she couldn't pretend that the world outside didn't exist for much longer. She was contemplating her next move when the phone rang.

"Good evening. I hope I haven't caught you at a bad time. I was calling to see if you could join me for dinner on Friday."

"I'd like that Frank, thank you."

* * * *

Penny had never intended to get close with Frank Ward and made it clear from the very beginning that she only wanted a platonic relationship. Over time, however, her feelings changed as she became increasingly aware of what a kind and thoughtful man he was. She'd been desperate to find employment, and was most grateful that Frank returned a previous favor by securing a job for her at Taylor Construction. Following a period of managing the canteen, she was asked to take responsibility for arranging entertainment of existing and potential clients. This subject had become increasingly important due to the company's rapid expansion. These new duties often brought her into direct contact with Alan Taylor. Sharing a flat with Daisy had given her the chance to observe his ways from a distance. Her initial concerns were only reinforced when dealing with him first-hand.

Despite Penny's bitter feelings toward Alan, she never mentioned them to Frank, knowing it would put him an awkward position. One evening over dinner, things changed in more ways than one.

Normally talkative and cheerful, Frank looked frustrated and irritable, which quickly registered with Penny. She placed one hand gently on his cheek. "What's the matter? You look troubled. I hope you know by now that you can share things with me, and they won't go any further."

Frank looked into Penny's eyes. "It's that bloody Alan Taylor. The man has no sense of decency and he doesn't give a damn about anyone other than himself. He's been that way since the beginning. God only knows why I've put up with it all these years."

"Has something happened?"

"Yes. Although it's probably best that I don't tell you the details. I suppose I shouldn't be surprised; he's been pulling the same old shit for years. For some reason it really got to me today."

Penny kissed Frank gently on the lips, "I've never mentioned this. I've known for twenty years that he's the worst type of a-hole."

Frank noticed a tear surface in Penny's eye. "What makes you say that? And what's upsetting you?"

Penny wiped her eyes with a handkerchief. "You know that miserable bastard didn't even show up for his mother's funeral. 'I had better things to do' was all he had to say when I asked him about it."

Later that night, Penny and Frank made love. For the first time, no money changed hands.

CHAPTER 23

"34 Hatton Gardens," Kate murmured to herself.

For several days, she'd been wondering how knowing Penny Trent's address may help her quest. She'd already concluded that getting closer to Alan Taylor or Frank Ward was highly unlikely. Probably her focus should be on Dick Casey, or now perhaps, Penny Trent. Kate was still mulling things over when her phone rang.

From John's tone is was clear that he was upset, "Can we meet at six-thirty?" he asked sharply.

"I thought we'd arranged to go out tomorrow night? Is something wrong?"

* * * *

Kate arrived at the Red Lion pub to find John sitting at a table looking glum. "I'm sorry if I was impolite earlier," he said, "No excuse, really, just that I've had a shocking day."

Kate kissed him gently on the lips. "I assume it's something you want to talk about?"

"Yes. It's almost unfathomable. This morning I received a call from Robert Davis. Naturally, I was excited at the prospect of meeting the operations director," John said, his face turning bright pink. "He told me the company had an important matter they wanted me to assist with. At first I was excited. That soon changed."

Kate was disturbed by John's growing anger, "What on earth happened then?" She asked.

"Apparently, one of our suppliers upset senior management. While he didn't mention names, my gut told me he was talking about none other than Alan Taylor."

Kate clenched her fists, and she felt her neck tightening. "Go on," she said softly.

"The supplier is a privately owned cabinetry firm. The plan they've concocted is designed to inflict a severe financial blow on the firm's owner. It's crude and nasty. Given what I know about Taylor Construction, I've no doubt it will be successfully carried out."

Kate experienced flashback's to her grandpa, "What are they plotting for heaven's sake?"

"They're going to award him a large contract, and then ensure he messes up."

"How can they do that?"

"Apparently, Taylor Construction has a 'plant' in his company, and they're going to use him to intentionally take incorrect field measurements. We will 'uncover' the mistakes following delivery of the manufactured products, refuse payment, and then sue the owner for negligence."

"Holy mackerel, but why was he telling you this?" Kate asked.

"They wanted me to take correct field measurements, so we can prove it was the supplier who screwed up."

"Wow, what will happen to the individual who took the incorrect measurements?"

"Naturally, he'll be fired, but Taylor Construction will take care of him, I'm sure."

Stunned, Kate struggled to find words. "What are you going to do about it?"

"That's no longer the question. I made my decision quickly and took the appropriate action." John said, looking forlorn.

"What did you do?"

"I told him I wasn't prepared to do something so obviously wrong and immoral. He said I had a promising career ahead of me and that I'd be making a big mistake if I refused to take directions from company executives."

Seeing John's eyes welling up, Kate leaned across the table and took hold of his hands. "Good for you, John. That was the right thing to do. How did it all end?"

"He said that if I refused to carry out instructions, he wanted my written notice immediately. It wasn't pleasant. He spat the words at me; he was really menacing. Then he handed me a pen and a piece of paper. His parting words were, 'You'll live to regret this stupidity, John Clark.' The look on his face was quite frightening."

John's distress caused Kate to conjure up a mental image of Alan Taylor. *First it's my grandpa, now my boyfriend, you bastard.* She knew there was only one thing that would permanently calm her inner rage.

* * * *

Kate assumed John would quickly find another job. He did respond to several advertised openings, but the end result was always the same. "I'm sorry. We've already filled the position."

"You just have to keep trying. I'm sure something will turn up soon," Kate said, when they met one evening to discuss his progress.

"There might be more to this than meets the eye." John said bluntly.

"What do you mean by that?"

"Well, think about it. I've applied for six jobs, all in junior positions. Why haven't I been called for a single interview?"

"Sorry John, I don't know where you're heading with this one?"

John sucked in his cheeks and his mouth narrowed. "I'm starting to believe it's those bastards at Taylor Construction."

"How could that possibly be?"

"Kate, while my time with the company was limited, I did work with a number of project managers and site foremen. Most were tight-lipped regarding senior management. But I overheard sufficient conversations to know it was not a good idea to mess with Alan Taylor or his henchman, Robert Davis. I suspect they can exert influence over other companies if they want to. I wouldn't be surprised if they've put me on the 'Don't Touch' list with local contractors."

"Surely you can't be serious. That sounds like something out of a James Bond movie. In any event, how could they do that?"

"Most local contractors belong to the same associations. I believe that if someone like Alan Taylor let it be known I was bad news, most would heed his comments."

"Do you really think he's that vindictive? I must say it's hard for me to believe he has that sort of influence. If you're correct, what are you going to do?"

"Good question. I only wish I had a good answer. I suppose one possibility is to look farther afield. I have to do something soon. I only have enough savings to pay one more month's rent."

Kate was at a loss, her emotions flowing between sympathy and anger. "I'm sure you'll figure something out," she said, giving John a hug.

* * * *

"I have some news I must share with you. How about dinner at Artie's this evening, and I'll foot the bill?" John said.

With the work day over, Kate rushed to the restaurant to find John already seated. "My nerves have been on edge all day. If you make me wait another minute I think I'll burst," she blurted out.

"I've been offered a job." He paused. "There's a complication attached to it."

"What kind of complication?"

"Maybe I should start at the beginning. Andy called this morning to tell me he'd heard there was an opening at his firm. He said they were anxious to fill the position, and if I was interested, their personnel manager would see me straight away. I went to his office immediately and discovered the position was in their International Division. The junior manager assigned to the project quit without giving notice, leaving them in a pickle. Because my experience fits their needs, he offered me the job."

"You've missed one important detail." Kate said.

"What's that?"

"Where's the project located?"

John inhaled deeply, "The British Virgin Islands," he said, waiting for a response that was not forthcoming. "Kate, I hope you know that the last thing in the world I want is for us to be apart. I'm getting desperate and I have to do something. If I do accept the offer, they promised me a permanent position in their London office when I return."

Kate broke her silence, "How long does the project last?"

"Approximately one year."

"Actually, there's another detail you've overlooked."

"Really," John said despondently, thinking he was making a mess of things.

"Did you accept the offer?"

For the first time, John relaxed a little. "No, I told them I needed to discuss it with my girlfriend. They do need an answer by tomorrow."

Kate tried to imagine a whole year without seeing John. She knew she'd miss him terribly. She also understood his predicament. Holding back tears, she said, "Well

John, when you get back I hope they're still called The *Virgin* Islands and not just The Islands."

John had grown to appreciate Kate's understanding nature and her occasional zany sense of humor. Though he was normally conservative in formal settings, without hesitation he leaned across the table and kissed Kate passionately. Relishing the moment, Kate hadn't noticed the server arrive with their food. When she did, she withdrew slowly and through a sweet smile said "Sorry to keep you waiting, miss. I hadn't quite finished the appetizer I ordered from my boyfriend."

CHAPTER 24

Arising early on Monday morning, Kate felt empty. The previous day, she'd driven John to London's Heathrow airport where he boarded a VC10 bound for Bermuda, the first leg of his journey to The British Virgin Islands. She'd been able to keep her composure until he disappeared through customs. Then the tears started to flow. She knew his absence would be difficult to deal with and hoped his promise to write weekly would prove comforting. She found some consolation knowing that she now had time to focus on another matter that she'd neglected since John's unfortunate departure from Taylor Construction.

* * * *

During a morning break, Kate's attention turned to Penny Trent. She decided that trying to orchestrate a meeting with Penny inside the office was never going to work. There seemed to be only one alternative.

On Saturday morning Kate got up at six-thirty and set off to 34 Hatton Gardens in her Morris Minor. Reaching her destination, she searched for a suitable parking space that provided a clear view of Penny's flat.

The longer Kate waited, the more her plan seemed flawed. By ten o'clock, she came to the conclusion that either Miss Trent had left for the weekend, or was staying indoors for the day. Thinking she'd only been embarking on a fool's mission, she started her car in preparation for the trip home. At the same moment, Miss Trent's front door opened. Kate's original idea was to engineer a chance meeting outside of Miss Trent's flat. That was quickly squashed when she saw Miss Trent run across the road just in time to board the bus that had pulled up.

Following the bus on its journey was simple. It made regular stops, enabling Kate to catch up if other vehicles separated them. Ten minutes later, Miss Trent disembarked in a busy high street. Then she crossed the road and disappeared into a department store. Wasting no time, Kate parked her car and ran back to the store, wishing she hadn't chosen to wear high heels.

The sign by the escalator indicated there were three levels. Kate guessed that Miss Trent was most likely clothes shopping, so she proceeded to the ladies' department on the second floor. Meticulously, she worked her way up and down each aisle, but there was no sign of Miss Trent. Deflated, assuming her guess had been incorrect, she walked back toward the escalators. In the process she passed the shoe section, where Miss Trent was trying on a pair of silver dress shoes. Doing her best to look like she was browsing, Kate picked up a pair of black high heels and sat in a chair opposite. She waited until she caught Miss Trent's attention, "We haven't met in person. Allow me to introduce myself. My name is Kate Elliott, and I work in the estimating department at Taylor Construction."

A wide smile appeared on Miss Trent's face. She'd been glad to learn that, at long last, a female was working in a management role.

"Of course, I've heard a lot about you."

Kate blushed. "Nothing too awful, I hope."

Miss Trent's warm laugh put Kate at ease and the two women engaged in casual conversation. Upon completion of her purchase Miss Trent asked, "Do you have any shopping to do?"

"No, I was just browsing." Kate said.

"If you have time, perhaps you'd like to join me for a cup of tea. There's a nice café just down the street."

Kate had conjured up an impression of Miss Trent that soon proved to be inaccurate. She was warm, engaging, and spoke easily on a range of topics. When it came time to leave the cafe, Penny offered Miss Trent a ride home, which she gratefully accepted.

"What a lovely surprise," Penny said, arriving outside her flat. "I really enjoyed meeting you. I'll give you my phone number, and perhaps we can have lunch one day?"

* * * *

Lunch with Penny resulted in another shopping expedition, which in turn led to evening dinners. The two women delighted in each other's company, and their friendship quickly blossomed, though Kate hadn't forgotten the underlying reason for making the acquaintance. At their get-togethers, she asked Penny the occasional work-related question, always being careful to avoid arousing suspicion of her underlying motive; though she knew that ultimately she would need to take a risk and push Penny a little further. She decided that Sunday lunch at an old village pub might be a perfect setting to do just that.

"I hope I don't sound nosey. How did you get your job, Penny?" Kate asked after they'd both ordered roast beef and Yorkshire pudding.

"Frank Ward introduced me to the opportunity. At first, I managed the staff canteen. When the company got larger, I was asked to take on new responsibilities. Now, I spend most of my time arranging entertainment for clients."

"So basically you work for the executives?"

"Pretty much, I suppose. Mainly Alan Taylor," Penny said.

"Is he easy to work for?"

Penny's reaction led Kate to believe she'd touched on a sensitive subject. "I suppose he's like most bosses." Penny said without elaborating.

Kate chose to switch subjects. She hoped the stage had been set to follow up the next time they met.

* * * *

Wishing to reciprocate for the Sunday lunch, Penny invited Kate for dinner at an upscale restaurant. On her arrival, the maître d' escorted Kate to the window table where Penny was studying the menu. "Good evening", Kate said, kissing her friend on the cheek and taking the seat opposite. When Kate looked directly at Penny, she noticed her eyes were a little puffy, making her suspect she'd been crying. She broached the issue delicately. "Is everything okay? You look a little upset."

Penny had hoped refreshing her face powder and lipstick would hide her outburst from earlier in the evening. "Oh, it's nothing sweetheart, just me being silly." She said, trying to make light of the matter.

"Are you sure? Is it anything you'd like to talk about?" Kate asked, and with that a tear rolled down Penny's cheek.

Penny blushed, "Can I tell you something in confidence?"

"Of course, you can count on it."

"I'd prefer to avoid going into details. I've known Alan Taylor for a long time. I don't want to say much more other than to tell you he can be very difficult."

"I assume it was him who upset you," Kate said sympathetically.

Penny's eyes filled, "Yes, he did. And not for the first time, I might add."

"I'm so sorry," Kate said, reaching across the table and gently squeezing Penny's hands.

Kate noticed that Penny was trembling. Though she felt badly for her new friend, her instincts told her this might be a perfect time to seize the moment. "I'm sure this will surprise you, Penny. I've known for several years what a nasty piece of work Alan Taylor is."

Penny's expression changed to one of amazement. Kate knew that what she was about to say backfire, but it seemed worth the risk. "Let me tell you two stories about Alan Taylor," Kate began. "The most pertinent one concerns my grandpa. The other has to do with my boyfriend."

CHAPTER 25

The Saturday following Kate's revealing evening with Penny, she arrived at 34 Hatton Gardens to be greeted with a glass of wine.

"Cheers," Penny said, clinking glasses. "I've had the opportunity to discuss things with Frank. He's been mad at Alan Taylor for years. The only reason he's put up with it is because he found himself unintentionally being a party to unethical and illegal activities, something Alan Taylor would hold over him if necessary. Recently, his tolerance level has been tested to the limit, and sharing your stories has put him over the top." Penny sipped on her wine. "He was unaware of the plan to deceive your grandfather at the time it happened. It was another one of Alan's devious moves. Furthermore, he knew nothing about the shenanigans with the cabinetry supplier. Robert Davis coordinated that."

"This doesn't come as a surprise. From what you've already told me, its clear Frank is not made from the same cloth."

"He was prepared to ride it out, given he's only a few years from retirement. Now he wants Alan to pay the piper. Interestingly enough, he's come up with an idea." Penny's eyes narrowed, "There's a certain irony about this because Frank was inspired by one of Alan's past schemes. Now, Kate, I must forewarn you that there is no guarantee his plan will succeed. Additionally, its implementation depends almost entirely on you." Penny began to squirm. "What we have in mind will require you to do things that I'm sure you'll find both immoral and degrading. However, we have to remember who we're dealing with."

Kate's face tightened. "Don't worry about me. I can't think of anything I wouldn't do to nail that unscrupulous piece of shit."

* * * *

Kate spent all of Sunday running over the plan she'd discussed with Penny the previous day. She knew there were numerous ways in which it could fail. Whenever doubt entered her mind, she regained her resolve by conjuring up a mental picture of her grandpa. Sleep didn't come easily that evening, though she was wide awake on arriving at the office early Monday morning. With her daily work schedule organized, she phoned Dick Casey.

"Good morning, Kate, what can I do for you?"

"I was wondering if you had a few minutes to meet. It's not urgent, just a personal matter that I'd like to discuss."

Dick's ears pricked up, "I can meet with you right now," he said. He would have found time to see Kate even if his day was full.

"Come on in," he called out when Kate's head appeared around his door. Dick had been attracted to Kate from the very beginning. While she hadn't reacted to his suggestions the way he wished, he hadn't given up hope that someday he might have an opportunity to further their relationship.

Kate closed the door and took a seat. "Over the weekend, I realized my second anniversary with the company was coming up later this year. The time has passed quickly, no doubt because I've enjoyed my work. That made me think how much I owe to you. First of all, having the courage to employ a female with no experience, and secondly, for all your support since then."

Dick was beaming, and Kate knew he was lapping up her compliments.

"I'd like to take you out for lunch, or perhaps dinner? I thought that might be the most appropriate way of saying thank you. It would be my treat, of course."

"That is nice of you, Kate, I'd love to. Do you have a day in mind?"

"I'm pretty flexible. Any day this week would work."

"Let's make it on Wednesday for dinner," he said, thinking an evening event would give them more time together.

"Anything in particular you fancy to eat?" Kate asked.

"There's not much I don't like. Why don't you surprise me?"

"Okay, shall we go straight from the office?"

"Sounds great, then we can have a cocktail beforehand. That will be on me, of course," Dick said, making eyes at Kate.

In the process of taking her leave, Kate spun around. "Dick, I've just had an idea. This weekend I'm housesitting for a friend. If by chance you're available on Saturday evening, I could cook dinner for you." She smiled and added, "That's if you trust me not to poison you!"

The thought of spending Saturday evening with Kate was very appealing and Dick guessed there may be more than dinner up for grabs. He wasn't sure if he had family plans. He'd rearrange them if necessary. He smiled inwardly, knowing he could honestly tell his wife he had a business dinner meeting that may require him to stay overnight.

"If your cooking is anything like your estimating, I know it will be outstanding. What time and where?"

"Let's say six-thirty for cocktails, and we'll eat around seven. The address is 34 Hatton Gardens. It's close to London Bridge."

"I know that area. I'll soon find it," Dick said, scribbling the information onto his writing pad.

"By the way, do you have a favorite after-dinner drink?"

"I love Cockburn brandy, but don't go out of your way just for me."

* * * *

The balance of Kate's week saw her anxiety level increase, and she often had difficulty concentrating on her work. Finally, Friday arrived, and at five-thirty, she took off in the direction of Hatton Gardens where Penny was waiting to greet her. There, they carried out a trial run, hoping it would mimic the way they planned events would unfold the following evening. In the process, they identified several things that could easily go adrift. Kate knew she would have to play things by ear and react accordingly. Feeling she'd given all the help and advice she could, Penny gave Kate a big hug, wished her luck, and took off to spend the weekend with Frank.

An entire week focused on the upcoming Saturday left Kate exhausted. She prayed that an early night would re-energize her. Her nerves were jittery. She poured a gin and tonic, hoping it would calm her down. Doubt was raising its ugly head, but she wasn't about to back down now. The image of her dear grandpa was crystal clear in her mind, and thinking about his demise, fueled her determination.

A sound night's sleep restored Kate's spirit, and following a light breakfast, she headed for the shops, returning an hour later to begin dinner preparations. By two-thirty, everything was complete. It would only take one hour for her to get ready, so she decided to sit down and read.

At five o'clock, she fixed her hair, applied make-up, and finished dressing. At six-twenty-five, she slipped into her high heels, waiting anxiously for the doorbell to ring, which it did precisely five minutes later.

Terry Bush

"You look stunning," Dick said, walking through the door, a bouquet of red roses cradled in his arms.

"Why, thank you," Kate replied. "You look pretty good yourself."

Kate made Dick comfortable in the living area, pouring two glasses of wine and engaging in topical conversation. "I should get dinner started soon," she said, finishing up her drink. She refreshed Dick's glass then led him to the dining room.

They enjoyed gazpacho for starters, together with a romaine lettuce salad. For the main course, Kate served roasted lamb together with an assortment of vegetables, and accompanied by the Burgundy wine she'd decanted earlier.

"That was delicious," Dick said when the last morsel on his plate disappeared.

"I'm pleased. I hope you've saved a little room for dessert." Kate said, taking off to the kitchen and returning moments later with fresh fruit and vanilla ice cream.

"Shall I serve coffee in the living room?" Kate asked, "I think we'll be more comfortable in there."

Kate sat opposite Dick. She was well aware that the high-hemline dress she'd chosen displayed her thighs. She'd already learned that Dick wasn't very advanced in the subtlety department; his blatant gawking confirmed this.

Initially, they talked about the business. It didn't take Dick long to turn the conversation toward personal matters.

"Let's leave work for the office. I was hoping tonight would be an opportunity for us to get to know each other. And perhaps have some fun in the process," Dick said, raising his eyebrows.

"All right, there is one thing I'd like to ask you first."

"Go ahead," Dick said, anxious to move in a direction that matched his desires.

"It's something that's been troubling me for a while. A few weeks ago I met with a subcontractor who was familiar with the Crescent Street Project." Kate noticed her statement made Dick sit up and pay closer attention.

"He went on to tell me that something odd took place with the plumbing contractor, who subsequently went out of business. He wasn't able to provide details though I got the strong impression he thought Taylor Construction was the root of the problem. I know you worked on that project, Dick, so what really happened?"

Thinking the evening was going well, and optimistic it would soon advance to another level, Dick decided to deflect the subject and hopefully move on. "It's true the plumbing contractor went bankrupt. I don't know the details, either. It's ancient history, Kate. Why don't we leave business for the office and talk about us?"

Kate shrugged. "I happen to believe you know more than that. Perhaps it isn't important to you, but it's been bugging me." She folded her arms and pouted. "However, if that's all you've got to say on the matter, let's move on."

Fully aware that the evening had taken an unexpected turn for the worse, Dick attempted to get things back on track, "Is there any special man in your life?" He asked, hoping the question may grab Kate's interest and brighten her mood.

Bluntly, Kate replied, "No, there isn't."

"Perhaps you and I could see more of each other, then," Dick said, leaning forward and smiling.

"You're married," Kate snapped back, "so that would be improper."

"Legally, that's true. Emotionally, it isn't."

Kate shrugged, "What does that mean?"

"In a nutshell, I no longer care much for my wife, and I believe the feeling is mutual."

"Why don't you divorce her then?"

"It's not that simple. You see, we have three kids and they all depend on me financially. For the time being, I have to fulfill my duty," Dick said, hoping his words would appeal to Kate's softer side.

Kate perked up a little, "That must be a very difficult situation. Can I get you another glass of wine?"

"Yes, please," Dick replied.

Returning with Dick's drink, Kate sat beside him on the sofa and in the process their thighs touched. "Have I ever told you how beautiful you are?" He said, gazing into Kate's eyes.

"I think you're just trying to flatter me," she replied, drawing herself away.

"I really mean it," Dick said, subtly shuffling his legs closer to Kate's. When she made no attempt to move, he put one arm around her shoulders and kissed her gently on the lips. Kate allowed the contact to last for a few moments. Then she promptly withdrew.

Tick tick

Adopting an authoritarian posture, Kate said, "That's inappropriate behavior. You're a married man."

Dick was finding Kate's vacillating moods unsettling. At the beginning of the evening, he thought there was a possibility they'd end up sleeping together. Now, it seemed more likely that he'd be shown the front door, rather than the bedroom door. "Kate, for some reason that I don't fully understand, one moment we start to get close and then in an instant, we're at odds. If it's my fault, I apologize." Dick pursed his lips. "Maybe we could start again? It would be wonderful if the evening ended on a good note." He sighed. "To be perfectly honest, Kate, I was hoping we'd end up spending the night together."

Kate adopted a thin smile, "I've been agonizing over our relationship. Earlier, I also hoped we'd spend the night together."

Dick hung on Kate's every word. "What's changed? Or do you still feel that way?"

"I'm afraid not. You see, Dick, I'm not the type of girl who can make love to someone they don't trust."

Dick was agape. "I don't know what you mean," he said firmly. "You've known me for nearly two years. Haven't I always been open and honest?"

"Up until tonight, I believed you were. But you lied to me earlier, and that changed my feelings."

"I don't know what you're talking about. I haven't lied to you!"

"You intentionally avoided my question about the Crescent Street Project. I could see from your body language that you were holding something back. In my world, that's the same as telling a lie."

Dick's mind started to spin. The episode with Wilson Plumbing still bothered him. He'd only carried out instructions; he hadn't known the implications. He'd remained ignorant on the subject until Alan Taylor's secretary's retirement party. That was when, following a couple of cocktails, she provided background information on the unintentional role she'd played. He remembered Alan Taylor warning him to never tell anyone about his role. But that was years ago, and he began to wonder what harm could it do to tell Kate now? There didn't seem to be any reason that she would repeat it. Why should she? He didn't see how it could possibly benefit her to do so. In any event, he could always deny telling her if needs be. After all, it would be his word against hers, and he was her boss for Christ's sake!

"Look, Kate. I may not have told you all I know. If I elaborate, will it change your feelings toward me and allow us to spend the night together?"

Kate raised her eyebrows and smiled. "If you promise to take things one step at a time and don't rush me, I will. No doubt you've always known I had the hots for you. Please understand that, because you are my boss, I feel a little awkward."

Dick relaxed and then recounted the Crescent Street tale in detail, emphasizing he was an innocent bystander and simply a pawn in a high-stakes game. Having given Kate the information she'd asked for, he feigned a yawn. "I'm starting to feel sleepy," he said, while rubbing his eyes.

"Okay, I need to turn the bed covers down. I'll be back in a couple of minutes." Kate was in the process of leaving the room when she suddenly stopped, "Oh my god, I've forgotten something," she shouted out before disappearing into the kitchen.

"Here you go," she said on her return, "Its Cockburn's brandy. Your favorite after-dinner drink, I believe."

Dick was touched. "Cheers," he said, raising the glass and taking a sip.

"Are you ready for bed now?" he asked, placing his empty glass on the table.

"Yes, I am. Why don't you go and tuck yourself in. I need to tidy up the kitchen; I'll only be a few minutes."

When Kate entered the bedroom she expected to find Dick under the sheets. Instead, he was lying naked on top of the covers, his clothes scattered around the room. She managed to hide her embarrassment and return Dick's smile.

Kate removed her shoes. Then she slipped out of her dress and hung it in the wardrobe. All the while she could feel Dick's eyes tracing her every step. Returning to the bedside, she unfastened her watch, necklace, and bracelet, laying each of them neatly on the end table. "I just need to use the bathroom. I'll be back in a minute," she said, removing her bra and panties and playfully tossing them onto the floor.

Dick's eyes were popping out of his head. Just a few more minutes, he told himself. Then he'd be able to satisfy the lust he'd harbored since the first time he'd met with Kate.

CHAPTER 26

When Dick awoke it took him several moments to recall his whereabouts. Slowly, the vision of Kate's beautiful naked body came vividly to his mind. Overcome with desire he rolled over, expecting to embrace the young woman lying beside him, only to find the bed was empty. He tried to gather his thoughts. How long had it been since he dozed off? Had Kate even returned from the bathroom yet? He wasn't sure. Perhaps she'd gone back to the living room to collect something. No point in speculating he decided, easier to just get up and take a look. He climbed out of bed, and in the process he noticed his clothes were missing. He chuckled, thinking that Kate was turning out to be more of a tease than he could ever have imagined.

Opening the door to the living room, Dick's lust was reaching a new high. His beaming smile quickly turned to a look of horror when he saw Frank Ward and another man sitting on the sofa.

"Looking for these?" Frank asked, holding up Dicks' trousers and gesturing for him to take a seat.

Dick's face turned scarlet, and he started shaking. Frank stood up and introduced his solicitor, Leslie Farr. "I'll come straight to the point, Dick. You know all about the caper Alan Taylor pulled on the Crescent Street Project. We can prove his guilt if all parties involved cooperate. Because you are a vital part of the puzzle, we need you to testify."

Confusion paralyzed Dick's ability to think clearly. Had Alan and Frank fallen out? Was Frank trying to find where his loyalty lay? How did they know he was here, and where was Kate? His mind was gyrating with possibilities, though they all sounded bad.

Reasoning it best to say something, he muttered, "Frank, the Crescent Street Project was a long time ago. My involvement was limited to obtaining a bid from Wilson Plumbing and checking on their organization. I don't know anything more than that."

Frank was livid, "You're a liar, Dick Casey, and we can prove it."

"How can you do that?"

"Easy, I just spoke with Kate Elliott. I understand you told her the whole story last evening."

Dick was dumbfounded. Was this a set up? Had Kate tricked and betrayed him? If so, how did Frank get her to do it? He tried to make some sense out of the situation. Clearly, Kate and Frank had spoken, but how could either of them prove anything?

"I've no idea what Kate Elliott told you; maybe she was just making up a story."

Frank nodded at his solicitor, "Would you like to listen to your conversation with Kate Elliott?" Leslie Farr asked, pointing toward the tape recorder sitting on the table. Dick's chin dropped and his breathing became uneven.

"I assume you're ready to cooperate," Frank interjected, "however, you should also be aware of something else," he reached into his briefcase and removed a spool of film. "This shows Kate and yourself naked in the bedroom— something I doubt your wife would be happy to see." Dick groaned, and any remaining fight he may have had left in him evaporated.

Knowing he had Dick cornered, Frank adopted a more conciliatory tone. "Look, we're only trying to see justice done. I know you didn't initiate the fraud and were only carrying out instructions. Actually, none of us knew what was happening at the time. Alan Taylor set it up that way. He's a cunning bastard. Providing you fully cooperate, we'll protect you. Furthermore, when the trial is over, we'll destroy the film and the recording." Leslie Farr gave assurance that Frank's statement would be honored. "Given the circumstances, I want you to take an extended leave of absence. Notify the company that you have a family emergency. I will authorize paid leave. Also, don't attempt to contact Kate Elliott."

* * * *

The previous evening, Kate pulled up outside Frank's flat, where he and Penny were anxiously awaiting her arrival.

"How did it go?" they asked in unison as Kate walked through the front door

"To say I'm pleased it's over would be an understatement. The first part of the evening was like a chess match, one I wasn't sure at times if I could win. Eventually, I found a way to offer up fools mate, and he swallowed the bait. Not to suggest that the remainder of the evening wasn't terrifying." Kate took a deep breath. "I put the powder in Dick's brandy and made sure he finished drinking it. I know you told me it always worked like a charm, but I couldn't help wondering if there might be an exception. God only knows what would have happened then."

Kate writhed. "Undressing in front of Dick was the worst moment of my life. I had to keep telling myself why I was doing it. I knew if all went to plan, Dick would pass out shortly. I excused myself, pretending I needed to use the bathroom. Then I panicked." Kate cleared her throat. "I was petrified he may come looking for me. I locked the bathroom door and put my full weight against it. I waited for at least ten minutes before tiptoeing back to the bedroom. Fortunately, Dick was out for the count."

"Well done, Kate," Penny said, giving her a hug. "That was very brave. Of course, we always had confidence in you."

"I only hope the recording and the film are clear," Kate said. "It wasn't a problem to discreetly switch the machines on, though I was terrified that Dick might spot them. I have to hand it to you, Frank. You did a great job of disguising their whereabouts."

"There's only one way to find out if we've got what we need," Frank said.

"Yes," Penny interjected, "Frank, of course, you can listen to the recording, but watching the film is off limits—for you, anyway!"

Frank threw his arms in the air, "You spoilsport," he said, laughing. His comment lightened an otherwise tense moment and brought a broad smile from both women.

* * * *

Things moved quickly following Kate's Saturday night encounter with Dick Casey. With new evidence available, Frank's solicitor was able to persuade the police to re-open the case they'd previously dropped. It had taken all Kate's resolve to make it through the evening with Dick. Now she had another gut-wrenching task ahead of her which she chose to carry out one evening after dinner.

"Mum, Grandma—I'll do the dishes and make coffee. Why don't you retire to the living room, and I'll join you shortly? There's something I need to talk with you about."

"Do you think its good news?" Rita asked her mother when they were alone.

"I really don't know, dear. Perhaps she has received a promotion or maybe another job offer. You know your daughter, she's very responsible, so don't worry," Lilly said, sensing Rita's concern. "She'll be here in a couple of minutes, and then we'll find out what it's all about."

Kate appeared with three cups of coffee on a silver tray. She tried to relax, "There's something that I've been hiding from you for several years." Her mother's mouth fell open on hearing her daughter's words, and her grandma gasped. "When I tell you the whole story, I hope you will understand why. It all started during a visit to Aunt Sheila's house following Grandpa's passing." Kate struggled to control her emotions. "It was unintended, but I overheard Aunty telling her friend the circumstances surrounding Grandpa's death." Kate noticed her grandma's eyes filling with tears. "At that moment, I promised myself that I'd do whatever it takes to bring Alan Taylor to justice."

Kate went on to explain why she had chosen to attend a construction college and described the events and her actions that had brought matters to where they were today. By the time Kate had finished her story, Lilly and Rita's sad faces were replaced with looks of pride and admiration.

✻ ✻ ✻ ✻

Alan Taylor parked in his reserved spot and walked toward the lift that would take him to his fifth floor penthouse flat. While crossing the lot, he noticed two men walking in his direction. They both had a burly build and were wearing dark suits. "Are you Mr. Alan Taylor?" the taller of the two asked when he drew near.

Alan glared at the man. "Who wants to know?"

"I do," said inspector Richard Cummings, pulling his identification badge out from his pocket. "We have a warrant for your arrest, and I would appreciate you getting in the back seat of our car," he said, pointing to an unmarked blue Ford Cortina.

* * * *

While testimony from Arthur Thomas appeared sincere, it lacked incriminating facts, which was further highlighted under cross examination. Dick Casey's statements were potentially damning. He was the only person who knew the background logistics of the scam first hand. Alan's lawyer argued this was only circumstantial evidence and proved nothing. Earlier, Alan had testified that the signed contract was a result of open negotiations, certain Frank would confirm this. The key appeared to lie in Frank's hands.

After being sworn in, Frank turned to face the prosecutor who asked the usual preliminary questions, establishing his background and role in the firm. With that out of the way, he asked, "Mr. Ward, Mr. Taylor has testified under oath that you and he had open negotiations with Wilson Plumbing that resulted in the signing of a mutually acceptable contract. Is that true?"

Frank felt the muscles in his neck tighten. He made a circular movement with his head to relieve the tension, "No, sir," he said, causing a ripple of murmurs around the courtroom. The judge called for silence, allowing the prosecutor to continue. "Then would you kindly explain what happened?"

"It's true we asked Wilson Plumbing to review contract terms and consider a reduced price. It's also true that George Lambert was given time to think things

What crime ? Govt contract ?

over. However, when an agreement was reached, Mr. Taylor had his secretary take the documents away in order to type in the new price. That was when the drawing receipt was substituted for the one that had already been reviewed. Wilson Plumbing, and myself for that matter, were unaware of this." Frank's statement caused another buzz to resound around the courtroom.

"In your opinion, was Mr. Taylor's secretary a party to this fraudulent misrepresentation?"

"No, sir, she definitely wasn't. Mr. Taylor told her that if negotiations were successful he would ask her to type the revised price into new contracts. He gave her two additional copies for this purpose. She was unaware those copies had the updated drawing receipts attached to them that Dick Casey had delivered earlier."

The prosecutor looked smugly at his counterpart, "Your witness," he said.

Alan listened to Frank's testimony in a state of disbelief. He knew he'd been nailed and there was no way out. His inner rage reached a new high, and he promised himself that he would get his own back, no matter what or how long it took.

The judge spent less than two hours deliberating in his chambers, during which time he briefly conferred with the lawyer for the accused. Returning to the bench, he announced his decision. Alan Taylor was sentenced to ten years in prison, Lilly Lambert was awarded fifty-thousand pounds in compensation, and Frank Ward would remain managing director until the money due Mrs. Lambert was paid in full.

CHAPTER 27

Kate arrived home one evening to find a letter from John waiting for her. Since his departure, he'd religiously kept his promise to write weekly. His letters were always lengthy, often including photographs and the occasional poem. Receiving his correspondence was a great joy for Kate and it underpinned their relationship. In turn, Kate also wrote regularly, knowing John shared similar feelings. Two months earlier, she had informed him of Alan Taylor's imprisonment while avoiding mention of her involvement. She believed it would be more appropriate to explain the details when he arrived back home.

After kissing her mother, Kate flopped onto the sofa and excitedly ripped open the envelope. She'd barely begun reading when she let out a piecing shriek.

"What is it, Kate? Is everything all right?" her mother asked.

"Yes, yes it is. I'm sorry if I scared you. I've just received some wonderful news."

"Spit it out then, young lady," her grandma chimed in. She had a hunch of what was coming next.

"It's John. He's getting home earlier than anticipated. He arrives at Heathrow Airport a week from Saturday, and he's asked if I could meet him. If I reply tomorrow, he'll get it before he leaves."

"That is good news," Kate's mother said. She knew how much John meant to her daughter.

* * * *

Noon was approaching, and Kate had been staring impatiently at the customs exit door for nearly forty-five minutes. The crowd was thinning out, and she was beginning to wonder if John had missed his flight. Out of nowhere, he appeared pushing a trolley carrying two large suitcases. His hair was shorter than the last photograph she'd received, and the deep tan he was sporting made him look even more handsome. She ran toward him with total abandon and threw herself into his waiting arms. The ensuing kiss lasted until they both ran out of breath, and then John gently lowered her back to the ground.

"I've missed you so much darling," Kate said through tears of joy.

"Me, too, and one thing I know for sure is that I'll never leave you again."

Kate looked lovingly into John's eyes. "I've so much to tell you. I expect you're exhausted from the journey. Perhaps I should take you home and we can meet up tomorrow."

"Actually, I managed to get some sleep on the flight. In any event, I desperately want to spend the rest of the day with you. Why don't we find somewhere to get lunch, and then look for a place where we can talk in private?"

"Good idea. There's a hotel just down the road. We could eat there, and if the restaurant's busy, I'm sure we can find a quiet place in the lounge."

Kate was able to find a corner table where they ordered drinks and toasted each other while deciding on their meals. The waitress picked up on the occasion and let them be, apart from discreet visits to refill their drinks. Kate gave John the opportunity to finish describing all his adventures before raising the subject uppermost in her mind. "I'm sure you remember me writing about Alan Taylor's trial and subsequent imprisonment."

"Of course, and the slimy toad deserves it. I know, because there's no doubt in my mind he was behind that fracas with the cabinetry supplier, and that's what led to our unwanted separation."

John sensed a change in Kate's mood. It was clear she had something important to say.

"There's a lot more to that story that I haven't told you. I'm anxious to get it off my chest because it's something I've been harboring since we first met. I hope with all my heart you'll understand why when I tell you the background."

John looked bemused. "Goodness gracious, this sounds surreal. I can hardly wait to hear all about it."

Kate described the close and loving relationship she'd enjoyed with her grandpa, leaving John at a loss as to where the tale was going. His interest perked up at the mention of the Crescent Street Project. Kate continued putting pieces of the puzzle in place, explaining why she enrolled at the College of Building. John's bemused look slowly turned to incredulous, thinking there couldn't possibly be yet another chapter to this bizarre story. He soon realized his mistake when Kate relayed the details of her Saturday evening at Hatton Gardens and what transpired from that.

Having told her story, Kate was concerned that John might be upset at the bedroom episode with Dick Casey. Though she made it clear they didn't have any sexual contact, she avoided sugar coating her actions. "It must make me sound like a tart, but to achieve my goal and trap that pig, Alan Taylor, I was prepared to do almost anything."

At first, John was dumbstruck. Slowly, his face lit up. He leaned across the table and kissed Kate tenderly. "I love you, Kate. I must admit this all comes as a huge shock. Having said that, I think you're very brave, and I only wish I had half your guts."

Kate smiled serenely, "I love you, too, John."

John stood up and walked around to Kate's side of the table. He bent down on one knee. "Will you marry me?" he asked.

Kate covered her mouth with both hands and shook with excitement. "Yes, my darling, yes I will."

CHAPTER 28

When the steel doors slammed noisily behind him at 3 o'clock on a misty afternoon, Alan Taylor's nightmare became his reality.

The previous day, September 20, 1972, he'd been sentenced to ten years' imprisonment. Following the judge's announcement, he was taken to a holding cell in Wandsworth Prison where he spent a sleepless night. Over the next four days, he filled out countless forms and was subjected to a variety of tests. Then he was transferred to a low-security facility outside Birmingham, the assigned location for his incarceration.

He'd been able to spend a few minutes with his lawyer, who told him he'd review the case to determine if an appeal was feasible. In the meantime, he recommended that Alan focus on maintaining good behavior; this could significantly reduce the time he had to serve.

Uncomfortable from spending a night on a hard cot, Alan fixated on Frank Ward and the revenge he'd take upon his release. Then his thoughts turned to Dick Casey.

He didn't put Dick in the same category as Frank, but he would also pay a heavy price.

With the passing days, Alan became familiar with the monotony and drudgery of a prison environment and its stark contrast to the luxurious lifestyle he'd been enjoying for many years. His daily routine included mundane tasks—sweeping floors, washing dishes and cleaning toilets—which were always left in a despicable mess.

Each day, he was allowed one hour in the exercise quadrant, time he used to size up other inmates. Most were guilty of minor crimes and considered low risk for violent behavior or attempted escape. In Alan's mind, they represented life's losers and his feelings toward them were largely contemptuous. But he was careful with his interactions. He wanted to stay out of trouble and hoped some of them may make his stay more comfortable.

At the end of Alan's first month behind bars, he had two visitors. The first was his lawyer, who told him he couldn't find sufficient grounds for an appeal. This rubbed Alan the wrong way. Seething with anger, his face turning purple, he thumped the table with both fists and shouted through gritted teeth, "You're my fucking lawyer. I'm paying you a fucking fortune, so get me out of this fucking hell hole."

This outburst caught the duty guard's attention, and he sternly warned Alan that any further breach of etiquette would result in a loss of visitor privileges. Not wanting to antagonize the guard, Alan calmed down, and with nothing more to say, his lawyer left.

Next, Robert Davis arrived for his allotted thirty minutes. He started his brief on current events, but when he mentioned Frank Ward's name, the thunder in Alan's eyes told him to stop.

"Keep a careful eye on that fucker. My lawyer persuaded me to give him full authority to run the business until the Lambert's are paid off. One thing you can be sure of." Alan paused and his eyes narrowed. "When I get out of here, Frank Ward will regret the day he was born. I'm relying on you to look out for my interests. I promise I'll see you all right when I'm in a position to do so."

Robert nodded dutifully, saying he'd be back the following month.

Returning to his cell, Alan reflected on his business. He had no doubt it would suffer in his absence. He was hopeful it would keep going, and he'd rebuild it after his release. His attention turned back to Frank. He knew that he needed to be careful. There was plenty of time to plan something that couldn't be pinned on him.

Two months into his incarceration, Alan was subjected to an intense interview, geared to assessing appropriate measures for rehabilitation. He was judged to be low risk, making him eligible for assignment to projects outside the prison grounds. He'd no interest in escaping. That would be pointless if he wanted to get back to his company. His only incentive was to see life outside the prison walls and ease the boredom.

* * * *

A fellow inmate, Duncan Mitchell, had recently tried to befriend Alan. Duncan was short in stature with curly blonde hair and an electrician by trade. Though Alan found him to be an irritating individual, he remained receptive, thinking Duncan may be an asset in the future.

On a wet Monday morning in December, Alan was summoned to the office of the assistant warden. There, he was informed of his selection to join a work crew that would be building a shelter and public toilets in a local park. It was made abundantly clear this was a privilege that would be taken away immediately if all rules weren't followed to the letter. Security oversight would be provided by a guard and his deputy, while technical supervision would come from the Regional Park Services. The assignment would begin in the New Year. Alan thanked the warden and returned to his daily routine, pleased that for the first time since arriving he'd soon get the chance to see the outside world.

Two weeks later, Alan, along with twelve other inmates, boarded the prison bus that took them to the park. The guard reminded the work crew of expectations relating to behavior, performance, and attitude. Then he introduced them to the park service officer who would be providing technical direction and supervision. If necessary, the inmates would be supplemented by tradesmen from private firms. Construction had been underway for six weeks and was on target to meet the three-month completion schedule. The park services officer was pleased with the progress made and thanked the assistant warden. Having free inmate labor helped him meet his tight budget.

In the late afternoon of the following Wednesday, the crew finished their work and started boarding the bus that would take them back to the prison. Alan had spent the day digging trenches to house the electrical conduits that Duncan was installing. With their jobs completed for the day, Duncan noticed Alan was covered in mud. He told him there was a bucket of fresh water in the partially finished washroom if he wanted to clean up.

In accordance with mandatory procedures, the guard counted the inmates getting onto the bus, and established one was missing. He asked his deputy if he'd noticed anyone still working in the building. When he said he hadn't, they took off together to investigate. Entering the washroom area, they saw Alan's crumpled body lying motionless on the floor, and closer examination confirmed he was dead.

* * * *

An investigation into Alan Taylor's demise was conducted by the local police in conjunction with the prison doctor. It was established that Alan had been electrocuted, presumably, by a live conduit that was immersed in a bucket of water. Given that Duncan Mitchell was the project electrician, he immediately became the prime suspect. Duncan however, fervently denied any responsibility, pointing out he'd personally informed the crew he was installing live cable. Furthermore, he'd clearly marked his new character @ p. 273 ?

work with florescent safety warning tags. All members of the crew corroborated Duncan's story and confirmed he and Alan were friends, leaving no apparent motive for foul play. Following a vigorous investigation, it was determined that Alan Taylor's death was either a result of misadventure or possibly suicide.

*   *   *   *

Duncan Mitchell was born in South London in 1944. His father was a bus driver, and his mother worked part-time serving lunch at a school. Duncan was a kind and thoughtful boy, slight in stature and inclined to be timid. His older sister, Carol, loved him dearly and looked out for him as he was often bullied by tougher kids. At age fourteen, Carol started dating Clive Johnson, who also kept an eye out for Duncan. This was the beginning of a life-long friendship between the two young men.

Despite being an intelligent child, Duncan had an inferiority complex. To combat this, he got his thrills from stealing cars. He only drove a short distance before abandoning them, knowing that otherwise he'd soon be in trouble. He'd been stealing for nearly a year without consequence, but it was inevitable he'd ultimately get caught. The first time, he received a strict warning from the police, but this didn't have the desired effect. At age seventeen, following two previous warnings, Duncan was sentenced to six months in a juvenile detention center.

Having served his time, Duncan's sister and her boyfriend pledged their support and helped him enroll in an evening class to train as an electrician. For the next two years, Duncan managed to get his life going in a better direction. One evening, however, he couldn't resist the classic Bentley he saw in a local parking lot. This lapse resulted in a one-year sentence, and worse still, his parents finally gave up on him. On his release, his sister and her new husband, Clive, welcomed him into their home.

Tragically, he relapsed again, and was given four years for stealing an Aston Martin. His sister visited whenever possible, and he'd been looking forward to seeing her again. He hadn't anticipated the devastating news she brought with her.

Several years earlier, her husband had started his own business and strove tirelessly to support his wife and their young child. One evening, he attended an industry event where he saw Alan Taylor sitting at another table with his latest girlfriend in tow. Alan owed him money and had been stringing out a settlement.

In the course of the evening, Clive had a few drinks. This led to him talking in a manner that was not typical of his usual polite demeanor. "Hello, Alan. I see you can afford an evening out with a young tart. It's a shame you're unwilling or unable to pay my bills."

Alan glared at Clive. In other circumstances, he would have taken him into the back alleyway and kicked the shit out of him. Tonight, that didn't match the image he wanted to portray to the beautiful young woman on his arm, who he planned on bedding later that evening. The manager happened to be passing by and, picking up on the incident, escorted Clive to another area.

In the process, Clive called out," Taylor, you owe me a lot of money, and it's three months overdue. You're hurting my business. Do the right thing for a change."

Alan was furious. In retaliation, he concocted a plan to destroy Clive's cabinetry business, and shortly afterward, it was successfully implemented. Facing bankruptcy, Clive took an overdose of sleeping pills and passed away during the night.

CHAPTER 29

Penny was surprised to find Frank on the line. He'd given her the day off to take care of some personal matters, and they weren't due to see each other until the following evening.

"Hello, Frank, what can I do for you?"

"Can you meet me for dinner this evening?"

"I thought we'd arranged to meet tomorrow?"

"I have some news to share."

Something in Frank's tone made Penny uneasy. "Is everything all right, Frank?"

"Don't be concerned. It's a little complicated. I'd prefer to tell you in person rather than on the phone."

Frank's assurance hadn't stopped Penny worrying from the moment he'd hung up. When she entered the restaurant that evening, her nerves were on edge. "So, what's going on?" she exclaimed when the cocktail waitress headed off to collect their drinks.

The smile on Frank's face disappeared. "It's Alan Taylor. He's dead."

Penny froze. "What happened?" She finally managed to say.

"Based on the report his lawyer received, he was electrocuted."

"Was he, you know—murdered?"

"Apparently not, the investigation concluded that it was either an accident or suicide."

"I can't picture Alan committing suicide. He's not the sort!"

"I have to agree. I suppose it must have been an accident. But that's not the end of it," Frank said ruefully.

"There's more?"

Frank shook his head and raised his eyebrows. "Yes, and it's a real doozey. Let me start at the beginning. Alan's lawyer visited today to inform me of Alan's death. Naturally, he wanted my assurance that I'd continue managing the business, at least until all the legal issues were sorted out. It occurred to me that Alan didn't have parents or children, so I asked what would happen to the ownership of the company."

"What did he say?"

"He told me that although Alan never married, he did have a son—."

Penny jumped in. "Holy cow. He kept that one quiet. Come to think of it, I suppose technically that makes his son a bastard. Let's just hope he's not like his father. Who was the unlucky lady, anyway?"

"Do you remember the first typist we employed? Her name was Margaret Brown, and she was a pretty young girl."

"I vaguely remember the name, but can't put a face to it. Was it her?"

"Yes, it was. When Alan found out she was pregnant with his baby, he agreed to a small payment with the proviso that he had no further obligation. To protect himself, he had a lawyer write up an agreement, and he made Margaret sign it."

"That's bloody typical."

"Margaret's husband didn't believe it was his baby, so he left her. Because she wasn't able to manage on her own, she moved back in with her parents. When the divorce was finalized, she and her son adopted her maiden name."

"Wow, it sounds like a soap opera."

"Yes it does, but I think even an avid television fan would have a hard time believing the next episode."

Penny looked at Frank with great anticipation. "Do tell."

"She changed her name back to Clark, and by the way, her son's name is John. I've arranged for us to have dinner with him and Kate tomorrow evening in order to break the news. Clark Construction has a nice ring to it, don't you think?"

Penny's jaw dropped. "Gosh, life is just full of surprises," she mused.

Frank grinned. "Sure is!" he said, wondering what Penny's reaction would be when he presented her with the diamond engagement ring he'd purchased the previous weekend.

Derick Taylor — Daisey → strip

alan (corrupt)

george lombard — Lilly

Rita

Henry/Wilms phires george   Penny Trent

Frank Ward   Dick Casey

Clive & Duncan good friends —

Efficient story telling

Made in the USA
San Bernardino, CA
11 May 2017